THE CHOCTAW CODE

BRENT ASHABRANNER
& RUSSELL G. DAVIS

D1316623

A Division of BJU Press

Greenville, South Carolina

Library of Congress Cataloging-in-Publication Data

Ashabranner, Brent K., 1921–

  The Choctaw code / Brent Ashabranner and Russell G. Davis.

    p. cm.

  Summary: In the 1890s, after moving to the Choctaw Nation with his parents, Tom finds his friendship with Jim Moshulatubbee complicated when Jim is sentenced to death under Choctaw law.

  ISBN 1-59166-621-X (perfect bound pbk. : alk. paper)

  1. Choctaw Indians—Juvenile fiction. [1. Choctaw Indians—Fiction. 2. Indians of North America—Oklahoma—Fiction. 3. Oklahoma—History—19th century—Fiction.] I. Davis, Russell G. II. Title.

  PZ7.A796Ch 2006

  [Fic]—dc22

                                                    2006005645

Illustration by Robert Gunn

Design by Danieru Sato

Composition by Sarah Kurlowich

© 1961 Russell G. Davis and Brent K. Ashabranner

© 2006 BJU Press

Greenville, SC 29614

Printed in the United States of America

ISBN-13: 978-1-59166-621-9

ISBN-10: 1-59166-621-X

15   14   13   12   11   10   9   8   7   6   5   4   3   2   1

CONTENTS

The Choctaw Code is set in the Choctaw Nation, Indian Territory, just before 1900, when the people in that nation, which later became a part of Oklahoma, were making their last stand—a peaceful one—to maintain their own way of life.

CHAPTER 1

The train conductor barged into the coach and bellowed above the hiss and screech of the old steam high-wheeler: "Atoka in the Choctaw Nay-shun. Atoka stay-shun."

As the train braked for the station stop, Tom Baxter handed down the boxes and straw suitcases to his father Harvey, while his mother, Hannah Baxter, gathered up the hampers and jugs from which they had eaten and drunk during the three-day trip down from St. Louis.

A Choctaw Indian, disappointing to Tom because he wore "store clothes" and no feathers, shuffled toward the door of the coach, one arm raised to shield his face from the soot and dust that settled everywhere. The Missouri, Kansas, and Texas Railroad—called the "Katy" by everyone in Indian Territory—was not the most comfortable railroad, Tom Baxter had to admit, even if his father did work for it.

They moved toward the door, and Harvey Baxter grinned back over one of his broad shoulders. "How do I look, Tom?" he asked. "Fit to be the new stationmaster?"

Tom grinned too and said, "You look fine, Pa."

In front of them a big man lifted a heavy, handsome saddle to his shoulder and moved out onto the platform. The big man's coat swung open, and Tom could see a holstered Colt and a belt heavy with cartridges. Hannah Baxter stiffened at the sight of the gun, but Harvey Baxter just winked

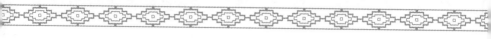

at Tom. Mr. Baxter had been a sergeant in an Ohio line regiment during the War between the States, and Tom knew he wasn't bothered by the sight of a gun.

Tom didn't know quite what to expect down in Indian Territory. All he knew about "the Territory" was what they said back in St. Louis. Some people said that it was fine country where the Choctaws, one of the Five Civilized Tribes, worked and farmed and ran their own schools and government. Others said it was just a hideout for bad Indians and the worst white outlaws in the West. They said that only Judge Parker—the "hanging judge" up at Fort Smith—and his marshals kept the country from running red with blood. Tom didn't know what to believe.

From the high step of the train, Tom got his first good look at the hills above the town. They were something to see. It was early summer, and the hills were a blend of every shade of green that Tom could imagine. They looked wild and rugged, and Tom figured they were full of caves and streams and all kinds of animals.

Tom's legs were stiff from the days of train travel. "I'd like to climb right up to the top of one of those hills," he said.

"I know what you mean," said his father. "You'll get your chance, and it won't be long."

The gun-toting stranger was also looking up at the hills, the way a man looks at his home, and he was sniffing the air. "Mighty pretty, the way them pines and oaks sort of melt together," he said to Hannah Baxter. He went on then, still carrying his saddle. Tom's mother smiled at last, perhaps thinking that a man who noticed such things couldn't be too bad, even if he did carry a gun.

As they drove in the railroad buggy out toward their house, the Baxters saw more of Atoka. Tom could tell that his father liked what he saw. There were several large white houses built in Southern Colonial style and some good-sized stores on the main street, but most of all there was space. Tom knew that for a long time his dad had wanted to get the family out of crowded apartment living in St. Louis and move to a place where he could be more his own boss. When the company offered him the job in Atoka, he hadn't hesitated for a minute.

Tom wasn't so sure how his mother felt, but he did notice her brighten when she saw the steeple of a freshly painted white church. Even though the streets were dusty and wheel-rutted and there were poor shacks in with the better houses, the church would mean a good deal to his mother, Tom realized.

Hannah Baxter's father had been a trader on the old Santa Fe Trail, but she had been born and reared in St. Louis after her father had started a trading business there. She set much store by "settled things" like churches and nice homes. Tom realized that she hadn't been sure about coming to the Indian Territory, but she had said nothing because she knew her husband thought it was the thing to do.

The railroad had a house for them at the edge of town, and they moved in that same day. The next day Tom's dad went to work at the station, and his mother started in to fix up the house the way she thought it should look. School was out in Atoka, so Tom didn't have much to do except take care of a few chores around their place.

On the second day he stayed around the yard, listening to the scream and howl of a nearby sawmill and watching horsemen and buggy drivers kick up dust along the road that ran past their house. After that he did move around the town a little, and he met two boys about his age. But after a couple of days one of them left to spend the summer with his grandparents in Ohio, and the other went to help his father in a lumber camp.

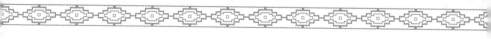

As soon as he had the time, Tom turned his attention back to where it had first been—the wooded hills that formed a half circle to the east and north of Atoka. He knew little about the outdoors, and at first he went into the forest cautiously. The hills were so thickly covered with oak and pine and all kinds of bushes that ten minutes' walking would take him out of sight of town.

In the beginning, he never went beyond the sound of the screaming saws and planers of the mill, but each day he went a little farther into the woods. Sometimes he took a sandwich and spent the whole day up on the pine ridges above the Muddy Boggy River. As he learned the landmarks, the cabins and clearings, the ridges and streams, he went deeper into the woods. It was still wild country. Near springs and creeks in small clearings were Choctaw cabins—mud-chinked log houses surrounded by small corn patches. Hogs and ponies ran untended through the thick tangle of brush and scrub oak near the cabins.

Tom always skirted the Indian clearings. It wasn't that he was afraid of the Indians, exactly. Most of the ones he saw from a distance were dressed in store-bought clothes just like all the other people he had ever known, though a few did wear loose shirts and leggings made of animal skins. The main reason for avoiding them was that, even if he could have talked their language, he wouldn't have known what to say to them. So he just stayed out of sight.

The days passed quickly in the forest although he could never quite explain to his folks what he did there. He didn't hunt because he had no gun and knew little about hunting. But he did watch deer and wild turkey, and once from a ridge he saw the back of a brown bear as it lumbered through a thicket below.

He didn't fish either. But the streams were sometimes very clear, and he would lie on a bank for hours, watching

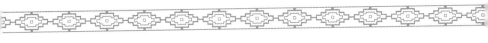

fish and turtles and other water creatures. There were berries of different kinds and colors in the woods, but, because he didn't know one from the other, he didn't pick any of them.

He was gradually getting to know the woods, and he wandered farther from the town. Then one day he got lost.

He had started out early in the morning and for some reason had forgotten to bring his sandwich after he had already made it. He headed straight for the ridges beyond the Muddy Boggy. Beyond the Boggy the Indian cabins were scarcer and not as well built as the Indian houses near town. Tom pawed his way through stands of scrub oak and toured around brush thickets that were too thick to go through. He had been keeping his eyes on a round-top hill that had one very tall pine on it. He was going to climb that pine and see if he could see all the way to Stringtown, another Katy stop not too far away.

The detours around the brush thickets threw him off. He had been hearing the sounds from the sawmill. Then he didn't hear them, but he did not know how long he had been going before he realized that the sounds had stopped. He decided that the mill had stopped for the noontime break. He doubted that he had gone beyond the sound of the saws.

The country was rough and a sea of growing things. He climbed a tree, but he could see nothing but the tops of countless more trees. He couldn't even spot his high pine or pick out the rounded hill. He could spy no farm clearings and no streams.

He shinnied down the tree and walked on, and finally he came to a tiny stream. He followed it, hoping that it would empty into the Muddy Boggy. It was rough going along the bank of the stream. Weeds and bushes and trees grew so thick that sometimes he couldn't see the water at all. Tom thought that the undergrowth of the African jungles couldn't possibly be any thicker than this. He kept as careful a watch

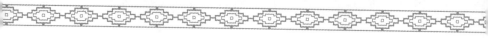

for snakes as he could because he had been told about the cottonmouth water moccasin that loved to lie along the banks of streams in these hills. It was poisonous, and Tom knew there would be no way to get help if he were bitten.

He stuck with the stream for about an hour, but it seemed to him that he was getting farther and farther away from the Muddy Boggy and Atoka. Finally he sat down on a log to rest and try to think of something else to do. But all he could think about was the sandwich he had forgotten to bring that morning. It was made of thick slices of home-baked bread with bacon, tomato, and a big slab of cheese inside. It sure would taste good right now.

Tom stretched out on the log and stared at the sun through the overhanging branches of a big cottonwood. He had learned to tell time pretty well by the position of the sun, and he judged it was getting close to two o'clock. He was lost, there wasn't any doubt about that; but Tom realized with a kind of surprise that he wasn't scared. He figured maybe he should be, but he was pleased that he wasn't. It put him on better terms with the forest somehow. All he could think about was how hungry he was, and the more he thought about that, the hungrier he got.

Suddenly his mood changed and he was scared. Or at least if he wasn't scared, he felt creepy, like something was going to happen. He sat up on the log and he shivered a little, even though it was very hot and humid in the undergrowth. He saw nothing and heard nothing, but he knew that something was different now. He noticed that it was quieter than it had been; there were fewer bird calls and no rustling noises of small animals in the brush.

Then, out of the corner of one eye, he was aware of something standing beside the trunk of the big cottonwood tree, something that hadn't been standing there a moment before. Tom turned his head slowly and gasped. A tall Indian stood there watching him silently. He was not more than ten feet away, yet Tom had heard no sound of his coming.

The Indian cradled a rifle in the crook of his arm. And he carried a stick with a dead wild turkey tied to it. The head of the turkey had been shot off cleanly. Tom sat frozen on the log, unable to move, his mouth too dry to speak. It was the Indian who spoke first.

"Something wrong, boy?" he asked.

His voice was deep, but not harsh. He spoke with an accent, but his words were clear. Although the Indian was not smiling, there was something about his strong brown face that looked friendly to the boy.

Tom stood up from the log. "Well, mister, it seems like I've got myself good and lost," he said.

CHAPTER 2

The Indian moved forward, rapidly and easily, scarcely making the turkey bobble on the stick. Tom thought the man was trying to get behind him, and he felt his stomach tighten. But then the Indian grinned and said, "How could you be lost? There's a path on the other side of those bushes."

Tom's stomach untangled. "It might as well have been a hundred miles from here for all I knew," he said. "I was about as lost as a person can get."

"You don't seem to know too much about the woods," the Indian said. "I've been watching you crash through the brush for almost a week now. You've scared most of the game clear up to the Cherokee Nation."

He laughed, showing white, even teeth. Tom stared at him. He was a person worth looking at. His shirt was of soft, fringed buckskin and finely made, though he wore regular store pants. He was not as tall as Tom had thought at first, but he was close to six feet and had wide shoulders and slim hips. Most of all he looked lean and hard and fast, just the way Tom figured a woodsman ought to look. And he was clean. He looked as though he had just stepped from a bath in the river; his dark hair was even freshly slicked down with water. Tom guessed that he was in his late twenties.

"Seen enough?" the Indian asked, still smiling.

Tom realized how long he had stood there staring, and his face turned red. "I'm sorry, mister," he said. "I guess I was just so glad to see you I couldn't help staring."

"That's all right, boy," the big man said. "You're new in these parts, aren't you?"

Tom nodded. "We've just come from St. Louis," he said. "My dad is agent for the Katy."

A shadow seemed to cross the Indian's face at the mention of the railroad, and he said, "Then your name must be Baxter."

"That's right," the boy said. "Tom Baxter. Do you know my dad?"

The big man shook his head. "No," he said, "but heard the name of the new railroad agent."

His voice came down harshly on the word "railroad," and Tom looked at him in surprise. "You sound like you don't like the railroad," he said.

The Indian looked up at the branches of the big cottonwood for a few seconds before he answered. "I don't," he said at last, "not even a little bit. But we can talk about that some other time. I bet you could use some food."

With just the mention of the word, Tom's hunger returned with full force. "My insides are just about to cave in, mister," he admitted.

"My cabin's not far from here," the Indian said. "Let's go eat." Then he added, "My name is Moshulatubbee. Jim Moshulatubbee. You just call me Jim."

He started out then and guided Tom around to a path that began on the other side of a thorn bush thicket. Once on the path, Jim Moshulatubbee really moved. In fact, it seemed to Tom that he fairly glided over the ground. Tom had to run to keep up, and finally Jim noticed this and slowed down.

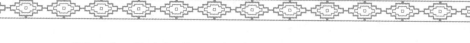

"You do all right for a city boy," he said. "No woods in St. Louis?"

"None I could get at," Tom said. "I hadn't seen half as many trees in my whole life as I can see here in an hour. I sure do like 'em."

Again a shadow seemed to come over the Indian's face. "I like them too," he said. "But they're being eaten up fast."

"Eaten up?" Tom repeated.

"By the sawmills in Atoka and Stringtown and other places," he said, "and being carried away by the railroad."

"But people need lumber, Jim," Tom said.

"I suppose," Jim said, "but why do they take the lumber from one place until they ruin it?"

Tom remembered then the large areas in the hills nearest town where there were nothing but stumps of great pine trees standing. It was an ugly sight, and the thought of all of these hills being that way made him feel pretty bad. But he couldn't think of a way to say this to Jim, so he kept quiet and walked along behind him.

They soon came to the crest of a hill, and in a clearing below Tom saw a cabin. It was a miserable, one-room shack made of slab scraps nailed together with almost no cutting and fitting. Board ends stuck out like bristles all over it. A wave of disappointment hit Tom as he looked at the poor place.

"Is that your cabin, Jim?" he asked.

Jim scowled. "Do I look like I'd live in a place like that?" he asked. "The Indian who lives there works for the sawmill in Stringtown. That's where he got his scraps to build with. No decent Indian would stay in a shack like that. That's the sawmills and the railroad again, making tramps out of the Choctaws."

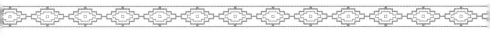

Tom could see that Jim was getting angry. His face was even darker than it naturally was, and his eyes flashed. But then he looked at Tom and saw that he was watching with a worried look; the Indian seemed to give himself a little shake, and a small smile came back to his lips.

"Well, there's no use fussing at you, boy," he said. "It's none of your doing. Say, can you hit anything with a rifle?"

"I don't know," Tom said, surprised at Jim's change. "I never have fired one."

Jim took his rifle from the crook of his arm and handed it to Tom. It was a Winchester .30-30. Tom knew that much. And it was beautifully cleaned and polished.

"High time you learned how," Jim said. "It's got four shots in it. See that patch of moss on the tree there? Reckon you can hit it?"

"I'd like to try," Tom said.

The Indian squatted down behind Tom and showed him how to jack the lever and throw a shell into the chamber, keeping the muzzle pointed up.

"Now," Jim told him, "just kneel down and hold it like this."

He managed to get Tom crouched down into firing position. "Don't be all tight," he said. "This gun only fires one direction—the way you aim it. Now line your sights, both of them, on that moss. Breathe in. When you let out your breath, squeeze the trigger nice and easy."

The rifle went off so suddenly that Tom jumped. The bullet chipped bark above the patch of moss. "You pulled up," Jim told him. "Now jack in another round and do like I told you. Don't let yourself know when it's going off."

Jim sat on the ground with his feet tucked under him and coached while Tom fired the other three shots. They were all

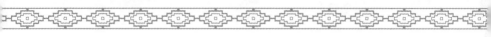

close to the mark, and the last bullet thudded squarely into the center of the small patch of moss.

"Good shooting," Jim said. "You'll learn, Tom. You'll do fine."

They went on and soon reached the clearing where Jim's cabin stood. It was a very different cabin from the one they had just looked at. It was good-sized and built of heavy, hewn logs, shaped and cut with an axe and adze. The logs fitted snugly and were chinked between. A mighty stone chimney rose above one corner. The roof slanted more sharply on one side than on the other, but there was no sag. The cabin had been well founded.

The clearing was as neat and clean as Jim himself. A small cornfield was enclosed by a brush fence. Hoes were stacked inside a lean-to shed, and a big tin tub hung by its handles. A water barrel stood on one side of the cabin door and a grind-stone on the other. Two good-looking ponies cropped in a stand of cottonwood at the edge of the clearing.

"Are you a farmer, Jim?" Tom asked.

"I wouldn't say that," Jim said. "I grow a little corn for myself, but mostly I just hunt and fish and trap in the winter to get what cash I need."

Jim peeled off his shirt and ladled water from the barrel into a wash basin. Then he lathered himself with yellow soap, rinsed off, and dried. Tom washed his face and hands but didn't bother to take off his shirt. He was too hungry to care much about how clean he was.

They went into the cabin, which wasn't locked, and Jim opened the shutters of the two windows. Light flooded into the cabin and showed it to be simply furnished but clean. Jim went to the fireplace, fanned the ashes off a bed of hot coals, and hung an iron pot on the spit over them.

"I'll just heat this venison stew now," Jim said, "but sometime when you come, I'll fix real Choctaw food."

While Jim was busy at the fireplace, Tom had a look at the cabin. It was one room but there was plenty of space. There wasn't much furniture: a table and two chairs, a bed in one corner, and a food chest near the fireplace. They all looked homemade, rough but solid. The floor was of hard, tamped earth.

On one wall Tom was surprised to see a shelf of books. Most of them were schoolbooks—readers, spellers, and an English-Choctaw dictionary. There was also a Bible.

From behind him Jim said, "Surprised to see an Indian with books? I can read 'em. I went to Spencer Academy after my folks died. I learned there."

Jim set two bowls of stew and a plate of cold cornbread on the table, and Tom pitched right in. If he had ever eaten food that tasted as good, he couldn't remember where. The stew was full of chunks of tender deer meat, and there were potatoes and onions swimming in the gravy. Tom cleaned out the bowl in a hurry and pushed cornbread around in it to get the last of the gravy. Jim smiled and refilled Tom's bowl, then settled down again to his own stew.

Tom finished his second bowl and, pushing back from the table, let his belt out a notch. "I don't think I'll eat again for a week," he said.

Jim laughed. "Well, not before tonight anyway."

He gathered up the dishes and started outside with them, but just before he reached the door, he stopped and stood very still for a few seconds. His head was slightly bowed and he seemed to be listening intently. He raised his head and stared out the door, then returned to the table and put the dishes down.

"Tom," he said quietly, "go sit in the corner near the fireplace and don't move until I say to."

Tom felt his mouth getting dry again. "What's the matter, Jim?" he said, almost in a whisper. "What's wrong?"

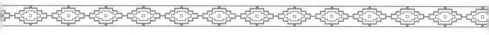

"Nothing," Jim said. "Just do as I say."

Tom went to the corner and Jim took his rifle down from its pegs on the wall. He moved carefully to a window, keeping near the wall. He knelt, edged the gun barrel a few inches over the window sill, and taking careful aim, squeezed off a shot.

The noise of the gun and a yell from outdoors blended together. Jim stood up, the rifle still at his shoulder, and said, "Come on out in the clearing, or I'll make the next shot count."

There was the sound of someone crashing through brush, and a man's whining voice said, "Now, Jim, hold it. I'm coming out."

Without turning his head, Jim said, "It's all right now, Tom."

Tom jumped up and ran to the window. In the middle of the clearing stood a short fat man with his hands held above his shoulders. He had thin red hair and a scraggly red beard. He was dressed in faded blue denim pants and a checkered red shirt, and they looked as though he had been sleeping in them for a week.

"I figured it was you, Welty," Jim said. "I saw you skulking down the Stringtown road this morning."

"Now, Jim," the man named Welty said, still whining, "that ain't no way to treat a person comin' to pay a friendly visit. You almost scalped me with that bullet."

"You were hiding in the bushes to see what you could steal when I left," Jim said. "Maybe you've forgotten that I told you to keep away from my cabin."

The red-haired man seemed to catch sight of Tom for the first time, and as if the presence of another person gave him a little courage, his whine changed into a sneer.

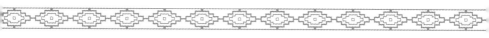

"You talk mighty big with a gun in your hands, Indian," he said. "It won't be long until you're looking into a gun barrel yourself. Then we'll see how tough you are."

A muscle jumped in Jim Moshulatubbee's jaw. "You've got five seconds to get out of here, Welty," he said. "And if I ever see you within a hundred yards of this place again, I'll put a bullet through your leg."

The man opened his mouth to say something else and then thought better of it. He turned around, hurried across the clearing, and disappeared down a path that led into the forest.

Tom felt his legs shaking a little from what had just happened. "Who is that man, Jim?" he asked.

"His name is Pete Welty," Jim said, "and he's the kind of cheap tinhorn that gives the Indian Territory its bad name. He makes his living sneaking whiskey in from Arkansas."

Tom knew that it was against the law to bring whiskey into any of the Indian nations. "Do you think Welty was really going to steal something from your cabin?" Tom asked.

"He's tried it before," Jim said. "That's the only reason he'd be hiding in the bushes here. The Choctaw sheriffs and the light-horsemen have been watching so close lately that he's been afraid to bring any whiskey in. That means he's looking for something to steal so he can turn it into a dollar. Come along. He won't be back."

They headed for town then, following the same path that Pete Welty had taken. They walked silently, enjoying the forest sights and noises, and before long they were within sound of the Atoka sawmill.

"I'll turn back here," Jim said. "You won't have any trouble getting in now."

"No," said Tom, "I've been on this path before." He paused and then said, "Jim, do you think I could come back

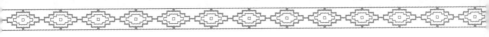

and see you again sometime? I'd like to try some Choctaw food and maybe go fishing or hunting."

The Indian smiled. "Sure, you can come back," he said. "You like the forest the way I do. I know because I've watched you. There aren't many people like you and me, Tom, not anymore. You've got the makings of a real woodsman."

Tom started off, happy with Jim's praise, and then he thought of something and stopped. "Jim," he asked, "what did Welty mean when he said that pretty soon you'd be look-ing into the barrel of a gun?"

Jim looked at Tom for a moment. He started to speak once but stopped himself and turned his eyes away to the trees, "Nothing, Tom," he said. "Welty was just talking crazy."

Tom didn't say anything else because he could see that Jim didn't want to talk about it. But there was something wrong; Tom could tell that.

He turned and walked down the path to Atoka with the feeling that something bad was hanging over his new friend.

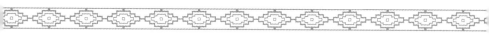

CHAPTER 3

Jim was right. Tom was plenty hungry when suppertime came around. While he ate, he told his folks about the day's adventures, toning them down a little for his mother's sake. He didn't let on that he had been quite as lost as he really was, and he didn't say anything about Pete Welty.

Still his mother fretted a little. "You say this Indian speaks English and can read?" she asked.

"As good as I can," Tom said, helping himself to green beans and potatoes. "Maybe better. And he's going to take me fishing and teach me things about the woods."

Tom decided not to say anything right then about shooting Jim's rifle and maybe going hunting with him.

"Well," his mother said. "I don't know about you running around the woods with an Indian."

Harvey Baxter smiled. "I would think that an Indian would be a pretty good person to be with in the woods, Hannah," he said. "Did this Indian tell you his name, Tom?"

"It was Jim," Tom said. "Jim Moshtubbee or something like that."

His father paused with his fork halfway to his mouth. "Was his name Moshulatubbee?" he asked. "Jim Moshulatubbee?"

"That's it," Tom said. "Do you know him?"

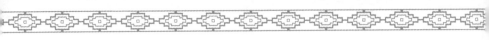

Tom was watching his dad, and he thought there was an odd look on his face.

"I've heard of him," Harvey Baxter said, "but I don't know him."

"I wish you would bring your Indian friend here to the house," Tom's mother said. "I'd like to see him."

"I'll try to get him to come," Tom said. "But I don't think he likes town very much. I don't think he likes the railroad either, Dad."

"Plenty of Choctaws don't like the railroad," Mr. Baxter said, "and they've got some good reasons, I'm afraid. I've found that out since coming here."

"What kind of reasons?" Tom wanted to know.

"The freight rates are too high," his father said. "Three times as high as they are outside of the Indian Territory. So are the passenger fares. And there are other things. I suppose I shouldn't be talking this way as a loyal employee of the Katy, but those things are true. It costs more to ride into the Territory than it does to go through to Texas."

"Jim doesn't like sawmills either," Tom said.

"Well, I don't guess you could expect a woodsman to like seeing his trees cut down," Mr. Baxter said. "Tom, the Choctaws are divided into two groups. They call themselves the Standpatters and the Progressives. The Standpatters want to keep the country just the way it has always been and keep the old customs. The Progressives want to bring in new things and new ways, even want to change the system of tribal landholding. It sounds like your new friend is a Standpatter."

The next three days Tom had to spend around the yard, weeding a vegetable garden plot and helping his mother set out shrubs and flowers. On the fourth day his chores were finished and he headed for the hills early in the morning. He

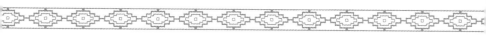

picked up the path to Jim's cabin without any trouble and followed it straight there.

As soon as he stepped into the clearing, he saw Jim sitting in the cabin doorway reading a newspaper. Jim raised his hand in greeting and said, "I was beginning to think you weren't coming again."

"I had to do some work around the house, but that's finished for a while now," Tom said.

When Tom came closer, he saw that Jim was reading *The Indian Citizen*, a paper published in Atoka. Tom had heard his dad say that it was the only newspaper in the Territory that stuck up for the Indians.

Jim stood up and said, "I was just about to take a walk in the woods. You want to come along?"

"You bet," Tom said. "That's what I came for."

Jim stepped into the cabin and returned with his rifle.

"You going to hunt?" Tom asked hopefully.

"No," Jim said. "I got plenty of meat right now. But I always carry my gun just in case something I specially want comes along."

As they started from the clearing, Tom said, "You ought to have a dog, Jim."

Jim stopped short, and his back went stiff. "Why do you say that, Tom?" he asked quietly, not turning around.

Tom was surprised by Jim's actions. "Why," he said, "I don't know. It just seems like a good place for a dog. He could guard the cabin and help you hunt."

"You didn't know I had a dog?" Jim asked.

"No," Tom said. "I haven't seen him."

Jim relaxed. "I don't have him now," he said. "He died."

"You could get another one," Tom said.

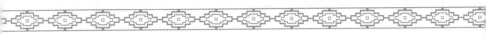

Jim didn't say anything. He moved on into the forest, and Tom followed him. There was no path, but Jim moved through the heavy underbrush as easily as if there had been one. Tom studied the Indian's movements and tried to copy them. And Jim helped him, showing him how to find holes in the brush where there seemed to be none and how to use his hands to keep branches from slapping him in the face and catching his clothes.

It wasn't easy, but after half an hour Tom felt that he was beginning to learn. He still felt clumsy, and he couldn't begin to move silently like Jim. But he wasn't getting slapped or stuck or tripped, and that was a big improvement.

Jim began to point out objects and name things. For the first time Tom learned the names of the trees he had been wandering through for two weeks. Jim named them all: hickory, sycamore, pecan, elm, maple, cypress. There were more oak trees than any other kind, and they had different names: pin oaks, white oaks, blackjacks. Tom didn't think he would ever be able to remember them all, or to tell them apart.

They came to some rocky high ground and started to climb over the tumbled boulders. "This is a good place to keep your eyes open," Jim said.

"Why?" Tom wanted to know.

Jim pointed to a rock about twenty feet away, and Tom saw a large snake stretched out sunning himself.

"Wait here," Jim said.

He made a wide circle and came up on a rock above and behind the snake. He moved noiselessly, and Tom saw that he had picked up a forked stick. With a quick, smooth thrust he jabbed the forked end just behind the snake's head. The snake lashed its tail and tried to coil, but it was firmly caught.

Jim motioned and Tom came over cautiously. "Take a good look at him," Jim said. "He's a copperhead. There are quite a few of them around here, and they love rocks."

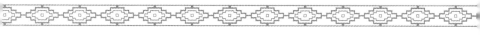

The snake was about six feet long and beautifully marked with a reddish-brown pattern.

"Is he poison?" Tom asked.

"He is," Jim said. "There are three poisonous snakes around here—rattlesnakes, cottonmouths, and copperheads. You'll find rattlers and copperheads mostly around places like this and cottonmouths along creek banks. Come on up here with me now and I'll let him go."

"Aren't you going to kill him?" Tom asked as he scrambled up the rock.

"No," Jim said. "They eat mice and other things that are nuisances. Besides, they won't try to bite you unless you step on them or try to catch them. They don't ever go looking for trouble."

He lifted the stick, and the snake immediately slid off the rock and disappeared into a crevice between two big sandstones.

Jim laughed. "He didn't like that, but he wasn't going to stay to argue about it."

They went on into another part of the forest, and in a little while Jim stopped and said, "Do you like squirrel?"

"To eat?" Tom asked. "I don't know. I never had any."

"Time you did," Jim said. "Nothing's better than squirrel when it's cooked right." He handed Tom his rifle and added, "See if you can hit the squirrel in that big hickory tree yonder."

Tom spotted the hickory tree right away, but he couldn't see the squirrel until Jim pointed him out on a high branch. Even then he couldn't see much more than a bushy tail, but he reckoned the rest of the squirrel was in front of it. Tom jacked a shell into the chamber the way Jim had taught him, raised the gun, and took careful aim. He tried to squeeze the

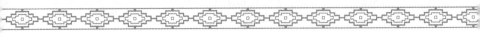

shot off nice and easy, the way Jim had told him to do. But in the last split second he felt his finger jerk just a little.

The sharp crack of the rifle seemed to fill the woods and bounce back from every tree. Tom saw leaves ripped away from a branch just a few inches above the squirrel's tail, and the squirrel vanished as if by magic into the safety of the green foliage.

Tom felt a sharp cut of disappointment at missing his first live target, but Jim said, "That was a fine shot. A squirrel is a hard target any time, and you dusted his tail with that bullet. You've got the makings of a real marksman, Tom."

Tom felt a lot better then because he knew that Jim meant what he said, and he felt really fine when Jim let him carry the rifle the rest of the way. It had a solid, comfortable feel, snug there in the crook of his arm. Right then Tom started thinking about the time when he would have his own gun, and he and Jim would go hunting together.

They saw no more squirrels on the way back to the cabin—at least Tom didn't. And if Jim did, he didn't say anything. Tom had the feeling that Jim was letting him do his own looking. They did come to a big berry patch, spreading under a stand of elm trees, and Jim stopped.

"Wild strawberries," he said. "Do you think your mother would like some?"

"I'll say," Tom said. "Strawberries are her favorite fruit."

"We'll have to get something to carry them in," Jim said. "You sample a few, and I'll be back in a minute."

Tom sat down and began stuffing the big red berries into his mouth. They were sweet and cool and the best he had ever tasted. In less than five minutes Jim was back, carrying two large, oblong green gourds. He whacked off the ends of the gourds with the skinning knife he carried in a sheath

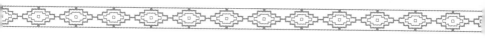

on his belt. Then he cut the pulp and seeds out of the inside, leaving only the hollow green rinds.

"Each one will hold a quart or more," he said. "Let's fill 'em up."

It didn't take long to fill the gourds with strawberries and eat all they wanted at the same time. They went on then to the cabin.

"Now," Jim said, "I'll fix us some real Choctaw food, and you can see if you like it."

The strawberries had sharpened Tom's appetite. "If there's lots of it, I'll like it," he said.

Jim smiled. "There'll be lots of it," he said. "I'm going to make *pashofa*. That's the Choctaws' main food. It will keep without spoiling for over a month, so we always make lots of it."

Jim went outside to the cool cellar where he kept meat, and came back with the loin of a skinned-out pig. "Got this pig yesterday," Jim said. "There are still plenty of wild pigs in these hills. The big ones can be mean, so you take to a tree if you ever see one coming at you."

Jim began to cut the pork loin into very small pieces, throwing them into a huge black iron kettle. He worked swiftly and skillfully, and the big piece of meat seemed to melt under his hands.

Jim finally got the meat diced up just the way he wanted it. Then he took a big basket of what looked to Tom like corn meal mush and dumped it in with the meat.

"This is corn that has been pounded until it's about as fine as meal," Jim said. "It's half cooked—I did that yesterday—and then dried."

Jim took a big, blunt-tipped pole and began to pound the corn and meat. He pounded and mixed, and mixed and pounded until the corn was beaten right into the meat. Then

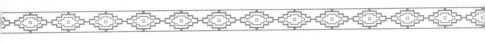

he hung the big kettle of meat and corn over the fire. He sprinkled salt into the pot and added quite a bit of water.

While the pashofa was cooking, Jim crushed strawberries and mixed them with a big yellow dumpling made of corn meal. Then he added cane syrup to it and stuck the pan at the edge of the coals to cook.

By the time the pashofa was done, Tom was so cramped with hunger that he could hardly get to the table. Jim heaped two plates with the meat and corn dish and set one of them in front of Tom, who pitched right in, although he was just a little disappointed because the food didn't seem to have very much taste. But the more he ate, the better he liked it, and he took a second helping almost as big as the first.

"Choctaws eat pashofa cold just as often as they eat it hot," Jim said. "It's just as good that way, maybe better."

"Couldn't be much better," Tom said contentedly.

Jim took the strawberry dessert from the fireplace and brought it to the table. "This is called *walusha*," he said, scooping a big serving onto Tom's plate. "It's the main Choctaw dessert. It's best made with wild grapes, but this strawberry mixture will have to do now."

It took Tom just one bite to see that it would do. It was smooth and rich and had a sharp flavor. It wasn't any better than the cobblers and fruit pies that his mother made, but it could stand pretty close to them, he figured.

When Tom got ready to leave, he picked up his gourds of strawberries. They reminded him of something. "Jim," he said, "my mother said she would like to meet you. Why don't you come into town with me?"

Jim shook his head. "I guessed your mother would want to see me," he said, "but not today. Maybe some other time."

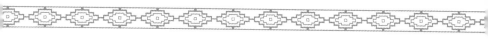

Tom's mother was pleased to see the big fresh strawberries that night, and when Tom started out for the woods again the next day, she didn't make any fuss at all.

Except for Sundays when he stayed home with his folks, Tom spent almost every day with Jim. They roamed the forest, fishing and hunting some, but mostly just walking and looking. Sometimes they rode Jim's ponies, and Tom got pretty good at bareback riding.

It wasn't long before Tom got his first squirrel. It was a clean shot through the head and maybe that was just a little bit lucky since he had aimed at the tail, but he was still mighty pleased.

Tom found that he was even more pleased at the things he was beginning to learn about the forest. He learned to tell the trees apart and name them without any trouble. He even learned what each of them was best used for. The forest was full of flowers and flowering bushes, and Jim taught him the names of them. Tom's favorite was the pink wild rose that seemed to grow everywhere.

Jim taught him about the different forest animals too and even showed him how to recognize the tracks that they made. It didn't take Tom long before he could tell a beaver track from an otter or mink track. And sometimes he could pick up the sign of a deer or a wildcat right in the middle of the woods.

Tom didn't think about it much, but in the back of his mind he knew that Jim was a great teacher. Tom was learning a lot, something new every day, and still having more fun than he had ever had in his life.

One day Tom had to stay home to weed the garden. He finished about midafternoon and decided to go to Jim's for a couple of hours. He went into the living room to tell his mother and found her drinking tea with Mrs. Bronson, the

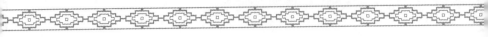

Indian agent's wife. Tom said hello to her and then said, "Mom, I'm going to Jim's for a while."

"Oh," Mrs. Bronson said, "I don't know any boy in Atoka named Jim."

"No," Tom's mother said, "it's Tom's Indian friend, Jim Something-or-Other. What is his name, Tom?"

"Jim Moshulatubbee," Tom said, because it was easy for him now.

Mrs. Bronson's cup clattered into her saucer. Her face turned white.

"Oh, no!" she said to Hannah Baxter. "You can't let Tom be around that terrible man."

Tom's mother looked alarmed. "Why, what's wrong with him?" she asked.

"My dear," Mrs. Bronson said, her voice rising slightly. "Jim Moshulatubbee is a murderer!"

CHAPTER 4

"Murderer!" Tom stared at Mrs. Bronson, who had clamped her lips tight after saying the word; but still the echo battered its way from wall to wall in the cozy room.

Finally Hannah Baxter spoke, and her voice was quiet but concerned.

"Whatever do you mean, Mrs. Bronson?" she asked.

"I mean that Jim Moshulatubbee killed a man," Mrs. Bronson said. "That makes him a murderer, doesn't it? He killed another Choctaw, and he has been sentenced to die."

Tom was shaken with hatred for Mrs. Bronson. Lights danced before his eyes, and he felt dizzy and then sick to his stomach. He found that he had been holding in his breath ever since the word had been spoken. He let out his breath in a rush. "That's a lie," he yelled. "Jim is a good man. He wouldn't hurt anyone."

"Tom," his mother said quietly, "you know better than to talk that way."

"I'm sorry," Tom said. He turned quickly and went to his room.

His mother and Mrs. Bronson went on talking, and Tom tried to listen, but he couldn't make out what they were saying. They talked for a long time, and Tom knew that Mrs. Bronson was telling more lies about Jim. Tom still felt sick to his stomach, and his knees were trembling.

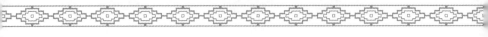

It seemed like hours before Mrs. Bronson finally went away, and just after she left Tom heard his dad whistling as he walked up the path to the house. Tom hurried out to meet him, and Tom's mother was there too.

"Well," Harvey Baxter said, "this is more welcome than I usually get."

"Dad," Tom said, "Mrs. Bronson has been over here telling stories about Jim!"

"Harvey," Hannah Baxter said, "have you heard anything about Tom's Indian friend Jim, about his getting into trouble with the law?"

Tom's dad fumbled his pipe out of his coat pocket but didn't light it. He wasn't smiling now as he had been when he walked up.

"Let's go in the house and talk about it," he said.

They walked into the living room and sat down. Fear knotted Tom's insides because he could tell from the way his dad acted that something was wrong.

"I suppose I should have told you, Tom," his dad said. "It would have been better than finding it out this way. I guess I kept hoping something would happen and you wouldn't have to know. It was the wrong thing to do, I can see now."

"Do you mean it's true?" Hannah Baxter asked. "You've known this and still let your son spend all of his time with a mur—"

Tom's dad said, "Now, Hannah, hush. Tom has had nothing to fear from Jim Moshulatubbee. I made very sure of that. The best men in Atoka—even the sheriff himself—told me it was perfectly all right."

Harvey Baxter came over and sat on the edge of Tom's chair and put his arm around his son. "Tom," he said, "do you remember on the first day you met Jim, I told you about

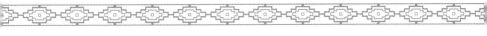

how the Choctaws are divided into the Progressives and the Standpatters?"

The heft of his father's hand on his shoulder made Tom feel better. He nodded. "Yes," he said, "I remember."

"Well," his father continued, "I was right about Jim. He is a Standpatter. At least he doesn't want the Choctaw laws about land ownership changed. Jim is a strong and brave man. You know that. He speaks right out for what he thinks is right. Jim has made plenty of Progressive Choctaws mad by telling them to their face that he thinks they are hurting the tribe. There are plenty of Choctaws mad at each other over this thing, and there have been some fights."

"I don't think Jim would pick a fight with anyone," Tom said.

"No, he didn't," Harvey Baxter said. "I got the whole story from the sheriff and the editor of the *Indian Citizen*. There was one man who especially hated Jim. I think he was a little jealous because Jim was a better ballplayer than he was, but the main thing was trouble over this Progressive-Standpatter business. This man poisoned Jim's dog, a fine hunting dog that he had had for years."

"Oh," Tom said, because now he knew why Jim had stiffened up so the day he had tried to talk to him about a dog.

"That wasn't all of it," Harvey Baxter continued. "The man bragged about killing Jim's dog. And one day when they met in Atoka, the man laughed in Jim's face and told him that if he got another dog he would poison him too. The man had a couple of friends with him, and I guess he thought Jim wouldn't jump him. But he was wrong. Jim couldn't hold himself back any longer, and he hit the man. They got into a real fight, and the man's friends ran off. Jim finally knocked the man down. When he fell, he hit his head on a rock in the road. It was one of those freak accidents. It killed him."

"But it was an accident," Tom said.

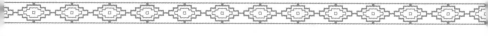

"Yes," his dad agreed, "it was an accident, but Jim had still killed a man. There's no difference between first degree and second degree murder under Choctaw law. He was found guilty by a Choctaw court."

Tom said, "Mrs. Bronson said that Jim has been sentenced to die. I know that's not true."

"I'm afraid it is true, Tom," his dad said softly.

"But Jim's not even in jail," Tom said. "If he had been sentenced to death, they wouldn't let him out of jail."

"That's something that couldn't happen in St. Louis or any place else I know of," Harvey Baxter said. "According to Choctaw law and custom, when a man is sentenced to die he may be given a year to live free. When the year is up, the man gives himself up to the Choctaw sheriff. The Choctaws don't believe in jails."

"But he could run away," Tom said. "Nobody would know until he was out of the country."

"That's right," Tom's dad said, "but if he believes in the Choctaw way of life, he won't run away. For him that would be worse than dying."

Hannah Baxter had listened to her husband without interrupting. Now she said, "I think it's horrible."

"I don't," Harvey Baxter said. "To me, it seems a whole lot better than keeping a man locked in a cell until he is executed. He has a year to live free, to make his peace with the world. A man can crowd a lot of living into a year if he has to."

"But Jim could still run away," Tom said.

"Yes, Tom, he could," his dad said, "but from what you have told me about Jim Moshulatubbee, I don't think he will. And I wonder if you would really want him to."

Tom went back to his room then. The knot was gone from his stomach, but he had a kind of dull, numb feeling

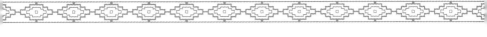

now. One part of his mind couldn't believe what it had just learned, but another part knew that it was true. Tom knew that his dad would not have told him the things he had unless he knew for certain that they were true.

Tom didn't go to the table when his mother called supper, and she didn't try to make him come. After a while she brought him a plate of food to his room.

"I know you're not hungry, Tom," she said, "but try to eat a little bit. The meat pie is tasty, and it will do you good."

"Okay," Tom said, "I'll eat some."

"And, Tom," his mother said, "I don't think you should go to see Jim anymore. You just try to forget about him."

Tom didn't try to argue. He didn't feel like talking at all, so he started eating. His mother left the room, and Tom picked at the meat pie for a few minutes but quit with most of it still on the plate. After a while he heard his mother and dad talking, and he opened the door a little.

"When will it be?" he heard his mother ask.

"Sometime in the late summer," his dad said. "In less than two months, I think."

Tom's mother said, "How will it . . . how will they . . ."

"By rifle shot," his dad said. "It's the Choctaw custom."

"I think it's horrible," his mother said again.

"Well," Tom's dad said, "it doesn't seem as bad to me as some other ways."

Tom closed the door and went to bed, but he couldn't sleep. He lay awake for hours trying to think of some way to help Jim. He heard the first roosters crowing before he finally drifted off to sleep.

Even so, he awakened early, got out of bed, and dressed quickly. He opened his savings box and took out all the money he had, almost five dollars that he had been saving toward buying a horse. His mother and dad weren't up yet,

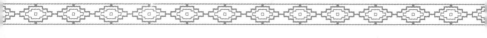

and he tiptoed through the house, carrying the five dollars in coins, tied up in one of his father's big bandanas. Five dollars wasn't much, he realized, but with money scarce in the Territory it would be some help to Jim. He closed the door softly behind him, sorry that he was going to have to disobey his mother, but still determined to help Jim.

The sun was clear of the treetops when he reached Jim's cabin, and Jim was sitting in the doorway tooling a slender piece of leather. Jim was skilled in leatherwork, and he made fine bridles and harnesses and belts.

Jim seemed to sense that something was wrong. "Panther chase you up the trail?" he asked, smiling.

"You got to get out, Jim." Tom held the bandana with the money in it and tried to push it toward Jim. "Take this. It will help some."

Jim frowned and drew his hand back from the money. "What are you talking about, Tom?"

"Take this money and clear out. I'll keep telling people in town that I'm coming out to see you. That'll give you a week or more. I mean it will be that long before they know you're gone. By then you can be out of the Territory and in Texas."

Jim smiled and shook his head. He said softly, "Tom, my friend, Tom. No one would try to stop me if I decided to leave. They'd just wait until I got back. And I'd come back."

"You've got to run away," Tom said. His face felt so stiff he could barely move his mouth to get the words out. "You can't just let them shoot you."

Jim stood up and began to whip one hand with the leather he held in the other. He muttered a few times, but nothing Tom could understand. "Tom, I want to explain. I want to and I don't know the words. I always hated men who could talk and talk, but now I almost wish I was one of them. Then I'd know what to say to you to make you know. I am a Choctaw, Tom, and I must follow the Choctaw way. The Choctaw code says I must not sneak away. I must use my year to live fully and right. Once the court sentenced me to die, there was no other way for me. My people believe that—I believe it. I lived my whole life believing it, and I'll die believing it. It can't be any other way, boy. It will come surely and in its time, as winter does when the fall has gone. I don't like winter, when the trees are old-looking, and the animals lose their flesh; but I know it has to come."

"But you didn't mean to kill that man. Everybody says that."

"But I *did* kill him. I was angry enough to kill him and I did. Choctaw law says that if you kill in anger you must pay this price. I'm a Choctaw. I've spent thirty years trying to learn how to be a good one. If I ran away, it would be against every tradition I have learned in my time. It would hurt and shame the other Choctaws—the good ones. And I'd always know. I'd always feel that I'd have no place to go. There is only one place for me to go, and I will when my time comes. That is sure."

"But, Jim—"

Jim smiled. "That's enough of this talk." He took the bandana from Tom's hand and stuffed it into Tom's shirt pocket. Then he handed Tom the piece of leather he had been working. Tom saw that it was a fine belt, decorated with all kinds of animal tracks—beaver, deer, muskrat, wildcat. Tom could recognize them all.

"It's yours," Jim said. "It's a memory belt. It will help you remember what they look like next spring when you go out again and I'm . . . I just thought . . . Today was the day we were going to hunt some deer."

Tom strapped on the belt. "Thanks, Jim," he said. "It will be a good memory belt for me. And it fits."

Jim laughed. "That's the way. Wait 'til I get my rifle."

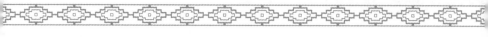

Tom waited outside the cabin door, half excited, half saddened by what had passed before. The thought of the deer hunt was strong. He had always wanted to go out after deer, but they had hunted only smaller things. Jim hadn't needed meat before, and he never hunted except when he did. Now the thought of getting a big forest buck helped Tom to forget about Jim's trouble for a while.

They walked a long way up into the hills that morning. They stopped once to eat some strawberries and another time for a cold drink at a clear-running spring inside a little sandstone cave. Then they came to a patch of thick scrub oak near a stand of young birch trees.

"We'll wait here," Jim said and slipped into the scrub oak. Tom followed him in. It was pretty scratchy, but it made a good hiding place.

Tom didn't know why Jim had picked that spot, but he found out soon enough. It wasn't long before a fat white-tailed doe poked her nose out of the underbrush. She trotted across a little clearing to the birch trees and began eating the leaves.

"Those birch leaves are tender and sweet," Jim whispered. "Deer love them."

"Why don't you get her?" Tom whispered back, fidgety with excitement.

Jim shook his head. "Never shoot a doe early in the summer," he said. "Her young will die too."

Jim had no more than said that when Tom saw another movement in the brush and out stepped a little fawn. Tom grinned. The little fellow was only about as big as a grasshopper, but it jumped around and butted its mother like it owned the world. It was fun to watch.

"I wonder if you could make a pet out of one of those?" Tom asked Jim.

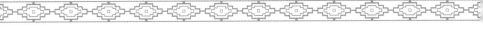

"They make good pets," Jim said. "I raised one once. Some hunter had killed its mother."

Just then the doe and her fawn trotted off. Tom and Jim waited a long time and nothing happened. Tom began to get restless.

"When you hunt deer, forget time," Jim said to him.

Tom settled back and in about half an hour there was rustling in the brush and along came a big buck. He was a beauty. With his proud head and ten-point antlers, he looked to Tom like the king of the forest. He walked over boldly and started ripping off the birch leaves. Jim whispered, "He's got a lot of horn for this time of year."

Jim raised his rifle and sighted along the barrel for just a few seconds. Then he squeezed the trigger. Sound cracked through the forest, and the buck lifted his head. He took one step and dropped in his tracks. Jim had made a perfect hit.

"By the next time, you will be ready to try for the big one," Jim said to Tom.

Jim took his knife and skinned out the buck right there. Then he cut up the meat and tied as much as they could carry on a pole. The rest he hung in a tree and said he would come back for it later. After that they each shouldered an end of the pole and carried the meat back to the cabin.

They fixed lunch and were almost through eating before Tom remembered Jim's trouble. It had been such a good morning that he had forgotten all about it. And he knew that was what Jim had intended.

As they were cleaning up the dishes, Jim said, "Tom, I'm a little surprised that your folks would let you keep coming here now that they know about me."

"Dad has known all along," Tom said. Then he figured he might as well tell the whole truth. "But Mom told me I shouldn't come here anymore."

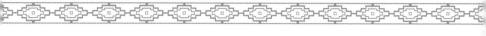

Jim smiled. "So you mind her by setting out bright and early the next morning," he said. "Didn't you tell me once that your mother would like to see me?"

Tom nodded.

"Well," Jim said, "suppose I go in with you today?"

"Good," Tom said, though in his mind he wasn't too sure what his mother would say, especially since he had gone to Jim's after being told not to.

On the way into town they did not talk much. Tom was busy trying to think of some way to explain to his mother why it had been necessary for him to go to Jim this morning and offer to help him. It was something he had just had to do. Although he felt this way, he wasn't sure that he really could make his mother understand.

It was late afternoon when they turned into Tom's yard and walked up the path to the house. Tom's mother was standing on the porch, and Tom didn't think that was a good sign. She was probably looking for him.

When they reached the porch steps, Tom found that all of the words he had been planning to say suddenly deserted him. He couldn't think of a thing to say but, "Mom, this is Jim."

"I'm pleased to meet you, Mrs. Baxter," Jim said.

Hannah Baxter looked at Jim, and Tom watched his mother closely.

Jim stood there, serious and at ease, a straight, clean-cut, well-groomed man. In the few seconds that went by, the expression on Hannah's face did not seem to change. But Tom knew his mother well, and he saw the little lights spring up in her eyes. They meant that she liked what she saw.

"I'm pleased to meet you, Jim," she said. "I've just baked some cookies. Maybe you and Tom would like to have some and a glass of cold milk."

Jim smiled. "I've never tasted cookies," he said, "but I'd sure like to try them now."

Tom felt a great surge of love for his mother. There had been no scolding, no reminders that he had disobeyed her. And in just a few words she had made Jim feel very welcome.

Tom grinned at Jim. "Wait'll you taste Mom's cookies," he said, starting for the door. "You'll think they're just as good as that walusha that you're going to make when the wild grapes come in."

Jim nodded and said, "I hope the grapes come in early."

CHAPTER 5

In the days that followed Jim became a regular visitor to the Baxter home. Jim said that he came mainly to get more of Mrs. Baxter's cookies, and Hannah Baxter always asked him to stay for supper and insisted that he take home some special treat like a part of a cake or a glass of jelly or a jar of preserves. Tom thought he saw another reason for Jim's visits—Jim had found another friend in Harvey Baxter. In the days in the forest it was to Tom that Jim talked, but at night, after one of Hannah's good suppers, Jim and Harvey Baxter had their talks. Tom would sit on the porch step and listen, interested but not saying much.

Jim had been a child during the Civil War, but everything about it interested him. Harvey Baxter, who had served through four years as a sergeant of the line, who had been wounded twice and promoted for bravery, was the man who could tell Jim about the things that interested him in the war. Even though most Choctaws had sympathized with the South and Harvey had served with the North, they rarely argued about the politics of the war. What interested Harvey most was *what* men did. What interested Jim most was *why* men did what they did in war.

But usually they talked about the Choctaw Nation and its problems. "I'm not really a Standpatter, Harvey," Jim said once. "I know things have to change; nothing ever stands still. I've learned that much from studying the forest. But I'd like to see my people keep their good customs, and I'm against two things—seeing the forests being cut away wastefully and seeing the Choctaw people cheated."

Harvey Baxter puffed at his pipe for a while before he said, "Like being cheated by the railroad?"

"That's one thing," Jim said, "and maybe the worst. It's not just being charged three prices for freight and train tickets, though that's bad enough. The worst thing is what the railroad is trying to do about land."

"I've heard it talked about," Harvey Baxter said, "but I don't really know what it's all about."

"Choctaw land is owned in common by the tribe," Jim said. "It isn't divided up in pieces and owned by individuals the way land is in the States. A Choctaw can have all the land he can use to live on and farm, and he can pass it along to his children. But he can't sell it. When he or his family stop using it, it goes back to the tribe."

"I understand that," Tom's dad said, "and I understand that the Progressives want to divide the tribal lands up and give a piece to every Choctaw to do with what he wants— keep it or sell it. You're against this, Jim?"

"Right now I am," Jim said. "Most Choctaws are still simple, uneducated people. There are a hundred ways they could be cheated out of their land if they had the right to sell it. It wouldn't be long before most Choctaw land would be owned by whites or a few smart, money-hungry Choctaws."

"How does the railroad come into this land business?" Harvey asked.

"When the Katy built through the Choctaw Nation, it was given a certain number of sections of land along the railroad right-of-way," Jim said. "The Choctaws didn't want to give the land, but the railroad demanded it and got it. The law says, though, that the railroad can't sell the land until

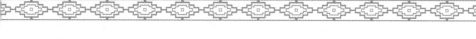

Choctaws have the right to sell their land. The railroad is itching to sell its land to white settlers. The Katy owners are doing everything they can to get the land laws changed. They'll do it sooner or later, I reckon."

Mr. Baxter said, "I work for the Katy, you know, Jim. But I hope you don't think I like everything the railroad does."

"I wouldn't be sitting here if I thought that, Harvey," Jim said. "The fact is, I've heard from the Indians around here that you're the fairest and best freight agent we've had in the Nation."

"Well," Harvey Baxter said, "I wouldn't know about that, but I thank you for telling me."

Tom's dad went hunting with Jim and Tom a few times, and Tom learned that his dad was a pretty fair shot himself. After a little practice he knocked a squirrel out of a tree and got a rabbit on the run. He brought out his big pistol from the war and showed he could still shoot.

"I grew up on a farm, you know, Tom," he said, "and I did plenty of hunting before I went to the city. Then in the war I got pretty good."

"Did you have your own gun?" Tom asked. "I mean on the farm when you were young?"

His dad grinned. "I did," he said. "Are you getting ideas?"

"I'd sure like to have my own gun," Tom said.

Mr. Baxter said, "We'll see. By real hunting weather this fall, we ought to be able to manage it."

It was only once in a while that Mr. Baxter could take the time to go hunting, but Jim and Tom continued to roam the forest almost every day. Sometimes they hunted and fished.

Sometimes they looked for honey trees. Sometimes they didn't do anything but walk or ride horseback through the woods. No matter what they did, Tom kept on learning about the forest and how to get along in it, and it was always fun.

Yet there were moments that were not fun. Sometimes as he watched Jim study a wildcat's track, or draw a bead on a wild turkey, or jump into Clear Boggy Creek just for the fun of being cold and clean, Tom would suddenly remember that it wouldn't be long before Jim wouldn't be doing those things any more. A chill would come over Tom then, and he could almost see Jim facing the rifle that would end his life. It was going to happen in less than two months now, Tom knew.

Whenever Tom had that thought, it hurt so bad that he just had to shut his eyes against the pain. It was at those times that he wanted to make Jim run away to a place where he would be safe. But the more he thought about it, the less sure Tom was that running away was the thing to do. He didn't want Jim to shame himself or his people. There just didn't seem to be any answer.

During the day when they were busy in the forest, Tom could usually forget about Jim's trouble. But there were those moments when he remembered, and there were the nights, after he went to bed. Then Tom couldn't forget.

Later in the summer Jim started teaching Tom something about trapping. They didn't try to catch any animals because their furs wouldn't be good at that time of year. But Jim showed Tom the best places to set snares and build traps, and he told the boy why they were best. Later he showed Tom how to rig a snare and how to build traps out of logs and tree branches. Tom made the traps over and over until at last Jim would say they were well done. Then he would start Tom on another kind.

They never talked about it, but Tom knew why Jim was teaching him about trapping during the summer. Jim wanted

him to be a good trapper, but when winter came, Jim wouldn't be there to teach him. When Tom first realized why Jim was teaching him trapping so early, he seemed to feel the biting winter cold in his very bones.

One day they came close to talking about Jim's trouble, and the talk reminded Tom that Jim was an Indian with an Indian's way of thinking. Tom had just finished building a practice trap, and Jim had looked it over and said it was good.

Then he said, "You're going to be doing that by yourself one of these days, Tom. You should build them just the same way you would as if I were with you. And you should hunt and fish just the same way. If you do, it will be good for me. But if you don't, it won't be good."

It was as though Jim were saying that even after he was dead, he would go on enjoying the forest and the things in it through what Tom did, if he did them right. Tom didn't understand the idea exactly, but in a way he did.

"I'll try to do all the things you've taught me, Jim," he said, "and do them right."

But just saying that brought a lump to Tom's throat and started him thinking all over again if there wasn't some way he could help Jim out of this trouble.

The very next day he got an idea of how he might. He had started out early for Jim's cabin because Jim had told him the night before that they were going to do something special the next day. Jim was waiting for him as usual, and they started off through the woods.

"Some of the people around here are getting together to catch fish today," Jim said. "I thought we would go and help them with the eating."

Tom had heard of Choctaw fishing parties and knew they were a favorite pastime, but he had never been to one.

It pleased him that Jim was taking him to a real Indian get-together.

They walked about five miles to Deer Creek, which was low on water and had some long, shallow pools in it. Tom had learned that pools like that usually had plenty of catfish in them.

There were already a few Indians in a clearing beside the bank, and others kept coming most of the morning. Sometimes whole families came in wagons with light canoes loaded in the back. Others came on foot or on horseback, and by about eleven o'clock there were over forty people there. They walked around and sat around and talked to each other. Most of them talked in Choctaw, so Tom didn't know what they were saying, but Jim took him around to meet the people, and they were all friendly. Tom noticed how everyone seemed to like Jim, and that made him feel good.

After a while the women and children started building a big brush fire. A few of the men brought bundles of dried roots, chopped them up, and began to pound them to a powder on a big rock in the clearing. Tom went over to watch, and he said to one of the men, "What are the roots for?"

The Indian smiled and said, "We catch fish with these. You watch."

When a good-sized pile of the roots had been pounded, the men took the powder and went to their canoes that were tied at the creek bank. They paddled to the pools, spread the powdered roots on the water, and came back to the bank. In a little while, fish began to float to the top of the water. There were little ones and big ones—some that looked like twenty-pound catfish to Tom—and they all just floated like logs. The men set out again and began to pick up the fish and put them in their canoes.

Tom ran over to Jim and said, "What's happening, Jim? Why are the fish acting that way?"

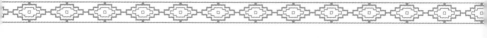

"Those roots that were put in the water are called devil's shoestring, Tom," Jim said. "They stun the fish so that they can't swim. It's an easy way to get a lot of fish in a hurry, and it doesn't hurt the taste of the fish."

Tom wasn't sure that he liked the idea of catching fish that way. "It doesn't seem right somehow," he said. "It doesn't seem like giving the fish a chance."

Jim smiled. "That's the way I feel about it," he said. "With you and me, hunting and fishing are more than just ways of getting food. But not for most Indians. The easiest way they can get their food from the forest is the best way for them. I can understand that. And they don't waste food. The fish that they don't pick up out there will be all right after a while."

Jim's explanation made it seem all right, and Tom went down to the creek bank to watch the men bring the fish in. He had never seen so many fish heaped up in one place when they got them all together. He was sure that there must be over a hundred two- and three-pounders, just the right eating size for a good channel cat.

The women took the fish, rolled them in mud, and stuck them in the coals of the big fire. Then they took long green poles, fitted them into Y-shaped supporting sticks at the edge of the coals, and brought armloads of ears of corn from the wagons. They shucked the corn and laid the yellow ears against the green poles to roast from the heat of the coals.

Tom could smell the roasting corn, and it seemed to him a long time before the food was ready. But when the call to eat finally came, he had to admit that it was worth waiting for. He cracked away the mud from one of the fish, and there was the tender white meat—moist, firm, and flaky. The hot browned corn was just the thing to eat with the fish, and before he was finished, he had eaten two whole fish and three ears of corn. The Indians sat around the coals, eating, talking, and laughing, and Tom thought it was about as nice a

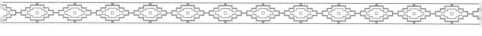

way for a bunch of people to spend the day as he could think of.

As the big meal neared its end, the sound of horses' hoofs came from the nearby trail, and after a moment three riders came into the clearing. They were all Indians, tall men who sat straight in the saddle and who looked hard and quick and strong. Each of them carried a rifle in his saddle boot.

Jim leaned over to Tom and said, "Light-horsemen. They're special Choctaw law officers. These three work for the principal chief himself."

Tom had heard of the Choctaw light-horsemen and knew that they were supposed to be some of the best lawmen in the West, but this was the first time he had actually seen one of them.

Everyone waved to the men and told them to get down and eat. The officers took the invitation, swung down from their saddles, and walked over to the food. One of them sat down beside Jim and Tom.

"Tom," Jim said, "this is Isom Kincade, one of the hardest riders and best rifle shots you'll ever meet, and a good ball-player too. I'll bet you've come all the way from Tuskahoma, Isom."

The big Choctaw bit into an ear of corn and said, "That's right, Jim, and we haven't done a bit of good."

"Looking for someone?" Jim asked.

Isom Kincade nodded. "Three whiskey runners," he said. "You probably know them—Pete Welty, Hiram Bragg, and Pliny Iskitima."

Jim made a face. "I know 'em," he said. "I hate to admit that a Choctaw could be fit company for those two renegade whites, but Iskitima is."

"They're slimy enough to slip by anyone," the light-horse-man said. "And they've sure managed to keep out of our way.

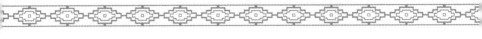

They were selling whiskey in Tuskahoma three days ago. We got their whiskey and smashed it, but they got away."

Jim went over to talk to the other two light-horsemen, and Tom moved a little closer to Isom Kincade. He was beginning to get an idea.

"Jim said you work for the principal chief of the Choctaws, Mr. Kincade," Tom said.

"That's right," Kincade said. "We take our orders from him."

"Who is the principal chief?" Tom asked. "What does he do?"

"Well," Kincade said, "he's the head chief of the whole Choctaw Nation. He's supposed to be the wisest one of us all and look after the good of the tribe."

"Can he change something that's wrong and make it right?" Tom asked.

"How do you mean, son?" the light-horseman asked.

"Like if something that is wrong was going to happen," Tom said. "Could the principal chief stop it?"

"Maybe he could," Isom Kincade said. "He's a powerful man."

Right then Tom made up his mind that he was going to see the principal chief of the Choctaws. He was going to ask the chief if he wouldn't do something to help Jim.

CHAPTER 6

From talking to Jim, Tom learned that the principal chief of the Choctaws was a man named Jonathan Wolf. He lived in Tuskahoma, the Choctaw capital, about sixty miles from Atoka. Sixty miles might as well have been six thousand as far as Tom was concerned. He didn't see how he would ever be able to go that far to talk to Chief Wolf about Jim.

And then, almost at once, the way came. One night Jim had come in for supper, and all of them were sitting on the porch afterward. Tom's dad and Jim were talking again about the Choctaw system of having all of the land belong to the tribe.

Jim said, "The Choctaw Council is going to meet in Tuskahoma this week, and the Progressives are probably going to try to get the land laws changed. I'm going there to talk against the change."

Tom's heart jumped when he heard that. "Jim," he said, "can I go with you?"

"Now, wait a minute, Tom," his dad said. "You don't just invite yourself along like that on a trip."

Jim spoke right up, "As a matter of fact, Harvey, I was going to ask you if Tom could come along. He's been asking questions about Tuskahoma, and I thought it would be good for him to see the Choctaw capital. We'll ride our horses, and it should be a good trip."

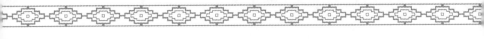

"Well," Harvey Baxter said, "when you put it like that—how long will you be gone, Jim?"

"Not more than a week," Jim said, "maybe less."

"I think it would be a fine experience for Tom," his dad said. "What do you think, Hannah?"

"I think so too," Hannah said, "but can Tom ride a horse that far?"

"Sure I can," Tom said excitedly, eager to stop any question about his going. "I'm getting to be a good rider."

Jim laughed and said, "He'll be a little stiff and sore when we get there. But he'll make it all right. There's no hurry, and we'll take our time."

"When do you want to go?" Tom's mother asked.

"Well," Jim said, "I thought we might start tomorrow after lunch and ride for just a few hours to sort of ease into the trip."

"Good idea," Harvey Baxter said.

"Jim," Tom said, "Mr. Wolf, the principal chief, will be in Tuskahoma, won't he?"

"He certainly will be, Tom," Jim said and added, smiling, "you have business with him?"

"I'd just like to see him," Tom said, knowing that he couldn't tell Jim that he did have business with the chief—important business.

Jim stood up to go. "I'll ride in about noon tomorrow and bring your horse, Tom," he said, "and we'll leave from here. I'll bring a cut of venison, Hannah, if you'll feed me lunch before we start."

"I'll feed you lunch," Hannah said, "and you don't have to bring anything."

After Jim had gone and they were getting ready for bed, Torn heard his mother and dad talking about Jim.

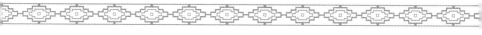

"He's an amazing man, Hannah," Harvey Baxter said. "In just a few weeks the Choctaw people are going to take his life, and yet he is going all the way to Tuskahoma now to make a speech about something he thinks will be bad for the Choctaws. Most men would be worrying too much about their own skins to even think about a thing like land laws."

Tom heard his mother say, "If Jim was worried about saving his own skin, he would have run away a long time before this. Yet no man can see his death coming and not want to avoid it. There must be times when he wants to run."

"I'm sure there must," Tom's dad said. "Choctaw honor demands a great deal of a man. But Jim believes in the traditions of his tribe. He'd rather die than dishonor them. I'd be the most surprised person on earth if Jim ran away before his execution day."

"He is a remarkable man," Hannah Baxter said. "I'm glad Tom has had a chance to know him."

"So am I," Tom's dad said, "very glad."

Tom lay in bed thinking of what he was going to say to the principal chief in Tuskahoma, but his last thought before he went to sleep was that he was glad he had the mother and dad that he had.

Tom was up with the sun the next morning to get ready for the trip. He laid out the clothes he wanted to take and rolled them up neatly in a couple of old blankets. When his mother got up she had him unroll the blankets and put in a few things he had forgotten like his toothbrush, soap, a pie tin to eat out of, and a knife and spoon. Even so, he was all ready to go by breakfast time, and it was hard waiting around all morning for Jim to come.

About ten o'clock Mrs. Bronson came to the house. Tom's mother invited her in and Tom tried to sneak out of the living room, but he wasn't fast enough.

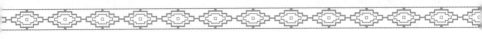

"Tom," Mrs. Bronson said, "I have a nice surprise for you. One of my nephews from Fort Smith is going to visit me this week. I know you will have a nice time with him."

Tom grinned. "Well, I'm awfully sorry, Mrs. Bronson," he said, "but I'm going to be gone this week." And then he couldn't help adding, "I'm going to Tuskahoma with Jim Moshulatubbee."

Mrs. Bronson gasped. "Whatever do you mean?" she said. "You must be joking!"

"No, he's not joking," Tom's mother said. "His father and I thought it would be nice for him to take a trip to the Choctaw capital."

Mrs. Bronson's thin face turned white and then red. "But to let him go with Jim Moshulatubbee," she said. "To let him go with a murderer!"

"Mrs. Bronson," Hannah Baxter said, "I know you are only trying to be helpful. But Mr. Baxter and I think that Tom is perfectly safe with Jim. We believe that he is an extremely fine man."

"Well," Mrs. Bronson said, "I never—"

"Excuse me," Tom's mother said, "and I'll get us some coffee."

The way she said it left no doubt that the subject of Jim Moshulatubbee was closed. Tom grinned again and slipped out of the room.

Mrs. Bronson left pretty quickly that morning, and toward noon Tom saw Jim coming up the road. He was riding the red roan and leading the little buckskin that Tom liked so well. He had a blanket roll tied securely around the roan's neck, and besides the cut of venison he had promised, he carried a freshly shot turkey, a gourd of wild honey, and another of blackberries.

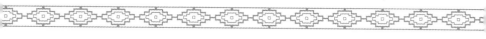

"Land's sake," Hannah Baxter said, "we'll never eat all of this without you and Tom to help us."

Jim laughed and said, "Fix some of it and give it to Mrs. Bronson. I passed her down the road a ways, and she seemed too upset to do her own cooking."

Tom's mother had a good lunch of stew and hot biscuits ready for them, and while they were eating, she asked, "Do you want me to get some food ready for you to take?"

Jim shook his head. "I've got everything we'll need, which isn't much. We'll depend on our aim and eat just like all Choctaws do when they're traveling."

They got started about one o'clock and rode up the regular road to Stringtown. It was only about seven miles from Atoka, but it was the first time Tom had seen the place. He didn't think much of it—just a sprawling place of sawmills, a train station, and false-fronted stores. There were no nice houses as there were in Atoka.

They didn't stop in Stringtown at all but turned right onto the Tuskahoma road. They climbed a good-sized hill just outside of town and followed the road, which led up a beautiful natural valley. Sometimes the valley narrowed down to a quarter of a mile and at other times widened out to four or five miles. But at all times the valley was surrounded by towering hills, hills so high that it seemed to Tom they should have been called mountains. They were covered with pines from top to bottom except for ugly gashes where the lumber camps had done their work.

Tom had done enough bareback riding, and the buckskin had such a smooth gait that he got along fine. Still, when they stopped at a spring about four o'clock to drink and to water the horses, Tom was ready to swing down and walk around a little.

When they started again, they left the road and followed a faint trail that Jim said was a shortcut. After they had ridden

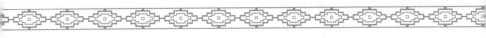

about an hour, they were well into the pine-covered hills, and Tom was a little surprised when they rounded a bend in the trail and came onto a small well-built log cabin. Jim called out in Choctaw, then dismounted and opened the cabin door, but no one was there.

"A friend of mine lives here," Jim said. "I'd like to see him, but we'd better ride for another hour before we make camp. Anyway, if my friend comes back to his cabin tonight, he'll pay us a visit at our camp."

"You'd better leave him a note," Tom said, "so he'll know you were here."

Jim smiled. "He can't read," he said, "but he will know I was here."

"How can he know that?" Tom asked.

"He's the greatest hunter in the Choctaw Nation," Jim said. "He can read signs like you can read a book. He knows my horse, and its hoof marks will be just like leaving a note saying I was here."

They rode on until the edge of the sun was resting on the western hills, and when they came to a clear, rocky stream, Jim swung down from his horse.

"Here's a good place to make camp," he said. He took a fishing line from his pocket and handed it to Tom. "You get us a good bass for supper, and I'll take care of the horses and build a fire."

It made Tom feel good that Jim would turn over the whole food business to him that way, and he felt even better because he knew exactly what to do. He took his jackknife and cut a willow sapling, shaved the small branches off of it, and tied on the line. Then he caught a grasshopper and stuck it on the hook.

He moved down the creek bank until he came to a little pool formed by three big rocks sticking up in the water. It

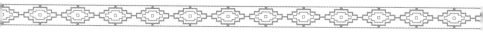

looked like a good bass hole, and Tom threw his line in by one of the rocks. It was only a couple of minutes before something hit the line and almost bent the willow pole double. He could tell by the way it struck that it was a small-mouthed bass because they had more zip and fight than any other fish he had caught.

He gave a quick little twist to set the hook, and then he pulled up fast and firm. The fish fought back, and Tom thought for a second the pole was going to break; but then the fish broke water, and Tom hauled him in. He was a small-mouthed bass and a beauty. Tom figured he weighed close to three pounds.

Tom had learned his lesson well from Jim about not being wasteful of any forest thing. But he knew how hungry he was tonight, and he figured that Jim would be about as hungry from the afternoon's ride. So he caught another bass, about a two-pounder, and then he went back to camp. He had done the whole thing in not more than fifteen minutes.

Jim looked up from the fire and smiled his approval. "Good work, Tom," he said. "Those two must have been waiting all day just for us to come along."

Jim gutted the fish and coated them with mud, and, when the fire had burned down, he placed them in the coals. When they were about ready, he went to his bed roll and took out a small package wrapped in corn husks. He cut the binding around the husks and took out a small brick of hard-looking, brownish material.

"This is *abunaha*, Tom," he said. "It's a kind of bread that Choctaws have always taken with them on long hunts."

Tom came over to watch Jim slice the abunaha. "It looks hard," he said.

"It is," said Jim, "but it's full of nourishment and it will stay good for a year. This piece is about eight months old."

"It looks like it's made with corn meal," Tom said.

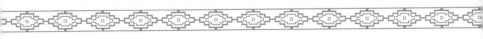

"That's right," Jim said, "corn meal mixed with cooked dried beans. The corn meal and bean mixture is wrapped up in corn husks, tied with hickory withes, and boiled in a pot of water for about an hour. Then it's just kept in the husks until it's eaten. It's sort of like hardtack. The kind your father used to eat in the war."

When Tom bit into a piece of the abunaha, it seemed rather tasteless to him. But the more he ate, the more taste it seemed to have, and it was good to eat along with the fish. Tom ate the bigger bass and Jim the smaller one, and then they built up the fire and spread their blankets on two beds of pine needles that Jim had scooped up.

But before they could lie down, the sound of a horse's hoofs reached them. The sound grew louder and Jim said, "That will be Gipson Bohanan, my hunter friend."

In a few minutes a shadowy horseman emerged from the fast-gathering twilight and rode into the light of the camp-fire. He stepped down from his big black horse and rushed to shake Jim's hand and throw his arms around him.

They exchanged greetings in Choctaw and then Jim said, "Gipson, this is Tom Baxter, a special friend of mine. We're heading for Tuskahoma."

"Glad to meet," Gipson Bohanan said and shook Tom's hand.

"Gipson doesn't speak much English," Jim said, "but he understands it pretty well."

"Pleased to meet you," Tom said, but it was not much more than a whisper because he was so surprised.

Gipson Bohanan was the biggest man he had ever seen. He towered a full head above Jim, but the real bigness of him was in his huge shoulders and powerful arms. Even in the dim firelight Tom could see the swelling muscles in his forearms. His hands were so big that Tom's own hand was completely lost in the handshake.

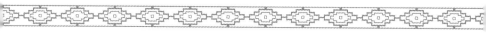

The hunter had a big head too, with long black hair and shiny black eyes. Across one cheek were three long white scars, running all the way from his ear to his chin.

They all sat down around the fire, and Jim and the big hunter talked for a while in Choctaw. Tom couldn't follow most of what they said, but he had heard enough Choctaw spoken by now to understand a little. He heard words like *isi* and *nita* and *nani*, which meant deer, bear, and fish, and he knew that Jim and Bohanan were talking about hunting and fishing.

After a while, Jim turned to Tom and said, "Gipson is mostly a bear hunter, so he does most of his work in the winter."

"Are there many bears around here?" Tom asked.

"Not as many as there used to be," Jim said, "but still enough to keep a hunter busy. Gipson spots their caves in the summer time, and then in the winter when they're hibernating, he goes in and gets them. Sometimes he gets more than one in a cave."

"That sounds pretty easy," Tom said.

"It is," Jim said, "but sometimes something happens."

Jim said something to Bohanan, and the big man laughed and nodded.

"You see those claw marks on Gipson's cheek?" Jim asked. "Well, once he went into a cave thinking he was going to have an easy bear kill. Instead, he heard a scream, and a full-grown panther jumped on him from a ledge inside the cave. I guess the panther thought he was trapped and decided to get first jump. He wasn't about to let go, and there wasn't any way Gipson could get loose. He had dropped his gun when the big cat sprang on him, and he knew he was in for a barehanded fight—him or the panther.

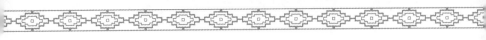

"Nobody knows how long they wrestled around in that cave. Gipson took a terrible clawing on the back and chest, and he got that mark on the cheek you see now. But finally he got his hands around the panther's throat. I found Gipson two days later lying unconscious in the cave. The panther was lying beside him. His neck was broken."

Bohanan had been listening intently and nodding as if he understood everything. "Much hurt," he said.

"He was hurt, all right," Jim said. "I nursed him most of the rest of that winter, but by spring he looked like he was ready for another panther."

After a little while Gipson Bohanan got up to leave, and they shook hands all around. Then after the hunter was on his horse, Jim walked a little way up the trail with him, and Tom could hear them talking. And it suddenly came to Tom that Jim was probably seeing his friend for the last time and maybe even saying goodbye to him now. That thought was a bad one, and it made Tom glad he was on his way to talk to the principal chief.

In a little while Jim came back, and they climbed into their blankets. Tom was stiff from the long afternoon's ride and plenty tired, but it was a good tiredness, and he was full and warm and happy to be spending the night in the forest with Jim.

He looked up at the stars for a while—a million bright dots against the velvety black sky—and tried to find some of the guide stars Jim had taught him. Then he closed his eyes and listened to the night sounds—the wind moving lightly through the pine branches, a fish splashing in the creek, a timber wolf howling at the pale half-moon.

"Jim," Tom said sleepily, because he wanted to stay awake for a few more minutes, "are wolves good for anything?"

"Not much, I guess," Jim said, "but they're not all bad. They're loyal and they have courage. I've seen a male wolf

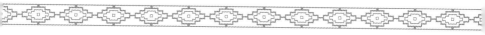

fight a pack of six dogs to give his mate and their whelps a chance to get away."

While the wolf howled, far off in the night, Tom began to drowse, and finally he slept. At first he was disturbed with confused dreams in which Chief Jonathan Wolf called to him from far out in the darkness. The Chief's voice was mournful and sorrowing, like the sound of a wolf, alone and without hope. Tom stirred in his blankets and came full awake, and Jim spoke to him, "Restless, Tom? Don't be. Everything is fine."

Jim's voice made everything seem all right again, and finally Tom slept without dreaming.

CHAPTER 7

Tom smelled the bacon frying before he opened his eyes. He lay in his blankets for a few minutes, warm and comfortable, listening to the morning sounds—the drilling of a woodpecker looking for breakfast bugs, the snuffling of the hobbled ponies as they cropped in a dewy patch of grass, the sizzling of the bacon in the pan.

He raised himself on one elbow and saw Jim hunkered down beside the fire slicing abunaha. When Jim saw Tom move, he looked up and said, "I thought I was going to have to wake you up. You must like sleeping outdoors."

"It was fine," Tom said, climbing out of the blankets and stretching.

"Bacon will be ready by the time you're washed," Jim said.

Tom would just as soon have skipped washing since he was camping out. But with Jim's reminder, he walked to the creek bank and splashed the stingingly cold water on his face and over his arms. The shock of it brought him sharply awake and ready for the day.

They ate quickly, rolled their blankets, and started down the trail. Tom felt pretty sore when his horse started jogging along, but after a while the soreness seemed to work itself out. About mid-morning they hit the road again and followed it through some of the wildest, most rugged country that Tom had yet seen. The hills were taller here—they were called the Jackfork Mountains, Jim said—and were covered with a thick tangle of oaks, brush, and vines until the pines took over on the higher slopes.

At noon they came to a rambling log building with a corral and windmill in back. "This is a stagecoach way station," Jim said. "A friend of mine runs it. We'll eat our lunch here."

They tied their horses in the shade of a huge elm tree and went into the stage station. It was cool and dark inside after the glare of the midday sun. On one side of the room was a long pine-board table with benches on both sides. On the other side were a few chairs where people could sit while they were waiting to eat.

They stood there for a couple of minutes, then a door opened and a small, gray-haired white man came toward them. Beyond the open door, Tom saw an Indian woman busy in the kitchen.

"Jim," the little man said, holding out his hand, "it's good to see you. You've stayed away too long."

Jim introduced the man as Charlie Thompson, and he and Jim talked for a while about Choctaw affairs and about the coming Council meeting in Tuskahoma.

"You've got to make a good speech before the Council, Jim," Thompson said. "What you say will go a long way toward holding the Progressives off on the land change."

"I'll do my best," Jim told him.

Thompson looked at Tom and said, "I'll bet you're both ready to eat. This isn't a stage day, so we don't have anything special fixed, but we'll do the best we can."

Charlie Thompson hurried back to the kitchen, and Tom said, "You'd think he was Choctaw, the way he seems so interested in Choctaw things."

"He is a Choctaw," Jim said. "He married a Choctaw woman and was taken into the tribe."

"I didn't know that could be done," Tom said.

Jim nodded. "It's been done quite a bit," he said. "Sometimes it turned out that the white men were just looking for good Choctaw land, but others—like Charlie Thompson here—are as fine as any people on earth."

In a few minutes Thompson and his wife came in carrying several bowls and plates, and they all sat down at the long table to eat. Their "best" looked plenty good to Tom—a big platter of venison steaks, corn pudding, and green beans boiled with bacon.

When they were about halfway through their meal, they heard horsemen ride into the yard outside, and in a few minutes the three Choctaw light-horsemen that Tom had seen at the fish-roasting came into the room. They all exchanged greetings, and the light-horsemen took places at the table. Thompson's wife went to the kitchen and came back with more food.

"Did you get Welty and those other two you were after?" Jim asked Isom Kincade.

"No," Kincade said, "and they're not worth spending any more time on. We need to get back to Tuskahoma."

They talked for a while after finishing their meal, and then Jim stood up. "We'll be getting along," he said. "See you in Tuskahoma."

Kincade nodded. "We're going to rest for a couple of hours before we go on," he said. "We've ridden from Stringtown without a break. I want to be ready to run in the big ball play."

"Is there going to be a ball game?" Tom asked.

"There sure is," Jim said. "You're going to get a chance to see a real Choctaw ball play in Tuskahoma."

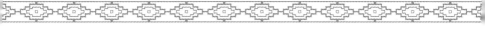

Jim and Tom rode the afternoon away at an easy but steady pace. The sun was getting close to the tops of the pines on the western ridges when they reached another clear-running stream. Jim turned his horse onto a path paralleling the creek bank, and in a few minutes they came to a small brush-encircled clearing.

"We could make Tuskahoma in a couple more hours," Jim said, "but it would be dark when we got there. It will be better to camp here and ride in, in the morning."

They set the horses to graze and made camp, Tom gathering wood and building a fire while Jim made beds of pine needles. They decided on fish again for supper, and Jim handed Tom the line.

"You catch 'em," he said, "and I'll go see if I can find us some berries."

Tom caught two nice channel cat without moving out of camp. He cleaned them, rolled them in mud, and put them beside the fire, delaying the roasting until there was a better bed of coals.

Shadows were settling over the camp when Tom heard Jim returning. For some reason Tom couldn't explain to himself, he felt a little troubled, as if something wasn't quite right—not just the way it should be. He stood up and walked around the camp. He paused and listened again to Jim's coming. And then he knew what was wrong. In all the time he had known Jim, he had never heard him make a sound when he moved through the forest. Tom turned to face the noise of cracking brush. Whoever was coming, it wasn't Jim.

This thought had no sooner flashed through his mind than the bushes parted and a tall, amazingly thin man stepped into the clearing. He wore a faded blue shirt too small for him and a pair of pants at least two sizes too big for him. His thick whitish hair stuck up in tufts, and his long nose looked as if a careless hand had stuck it there, not quite straight

on his face. He reminded Tom of scarecrows he had seen in cornfields around Atoka.

The man half turned into the brush and said, "It's just a kid here."

Immediately there was more noise in the brush and two more men came into the clearing. One of them was a short, powerfully built Indian, and the other was a fat red-haired man. Tom's stomach jumped when he saw this man. It was Pete Welty.

Welty blinked his watery blue eyes and stared at Tom. "I seen this kid somewhere before," he said. He came a few steps closer to Tom, and his mouth came open in surprise. "I seen this kid at Jim Moshulatubbee's cabin one day," he said. The two horses moved into sight among the trees where they were grazing, and Welty pointed to them. "Those are Moshulatubbee's horses. This is Baxter's kid."

Tom stood still, not saying anything, not knowing what to do. He knew that the two men with Welty were Hiram Bragg and Pliny Iskitima and that all three of them were wanted by the light-horsemen.

The sound of Jim Moshulatubbee's name seemed to bother Pliny Iskitima. "Let's get outa here," he said, his voice heavy with accent. "I'd soona meet the light-horsemen than Moshulatubbee."

"Moshulatubbee ain't here," Pete Welty said, and Tom noticed the same sneering note in his voice that had been there the last time. "And we need things to sell if we're gonna get money to get back in business."

Welty took a small gun out of his pocket, and Tom recognized it as a derringer. "I'll keep a lookout," Welty said. "You two get the horses and those blankets and anything that's wrapped up in them."

Tom had been on the edge of being scared, but the way that Welty talked about taking their things, just as if he wasn't

there, brought an anger to Tom that wiped out his fear and brought a pounding to his temples.

"You'll be sorry if you lay a hand on those horses or blankets," he said.

Hiram Bragg laughed and started across the clearing. "Talk like that can get you in trouble, kid," he said. "You can't back it up."

Suddenly the sharp crack of a rifle filled the clearing. Pete Welty screamed and the derringer flew from his hand. Blood spurted from his fingers, and he fell moaning to the ground.

Instantly, Pliny Iskitima turned and dashed for the bushes, but Jim moved swiftly into the clearing, caught the Indian before he was well started, and chopped the rifle barrel across his head. Iskitima fell heavily and covered his head with one arm.

Hiram Bragg grabbed for Tom as if to use him for a shield, but Tom jerked away and then threw himself in a flying tackle at Bragg's legs. The thin man seemed to fold up in sections as he spilled to the ground. Tom rolled out from under him and danced away, leaving Bragg in a tangle of his own arms and legs.

"Nice work, Tom," Jim said. "Throw some of that wood on the fire, then come over here by me."

Tom followed his instructions; then, one by one, Jim made the three men get up and lie face-down, side by side in the light of the fire.

"You make just one little move like you intend to get up," Jim said, "and you'll get a bullet in the leg."

"My hand is hurt," Welty moaned. "I'm bleeding."

"You're not bleeding enough to get excited about," Jim said. He turned to Tom and said, "Go out to the road and

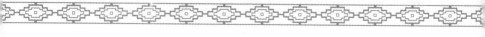

wait for the light-horsemen. They ought to be along real soon now."

Tom ran down the path to the road and sat down on a rock to wait. It was almost dark now, and he became a little edgy sitting there alone just waiting. He decided to build a fire to keep him company, and he had just got it going well when he heard the sound of horses in the darkness beyond. It was another five minutes before they came in sight, and Tom gave a sigh of relief when he saw that it was the Choctaw lawmen.

The light-horsemen drew rein and Isom Kincade said with surprise, "What are you doing here, Tom? Where's Jim?"

"Oh," Tom said, and he enjoyed making his voice sound like it wasn't much at all, "we caught those fellows you've been looking for. Jim's holding them back at camp."

"What?" one of the men said. "You're joking!"

"Come on," Tom said. "I'll take you to them."

He led them down the path to camp, and in ten minutes the three whiskey runners were tied and ready to travel. Welty was still whining over his hand, and Kincade tied a handkerchief around it.

"Well, Tom," Kincade said as they started out, "I guess we'll have to appoint you and Jim honorary light-horsemen."

Tom felt pretty proud then, but just at that moment he looked at Pete Welty and Hiram Bragg, and he saw the look of hatred on their faces. A little shiver went down Tom's back, and he hoped that he and Jim had seen the last of them.

CHAPTER 8

Jim and Tom took their time the next morning, getting a rabbit for their breakfast and having a swim in the Kiamichi
River, and arrived in Tuskahoma about mid-morning. As
they rode down the hills to where the town nestled in a grass-
covered valley, Tom thought it was one of the prettiest sights
he had seen in the Indian Territory.

"Jim," he said, "I've been trying to figure out what
Tuskahoma means. *Homa* is red in Choctaw, but I don't think
I've ever heard *tuska*."

Jim smiled. "Good," he said. "You're learning about
Choctaw names. You probably haven't heard tuska because
we don't use the word much any more. It means warrior."

"Then Tuskahoma means Red Warrior," Tom said.

"That's right," Jim said. "Choctaws like the name because it reminds us of the past when we were strong and
ruled ourselves."

"I thought the Choctaws still had their own government,"
Tom said.

"Yes," Jim said, "but every year we lose something to the
white men and the government in Washington. Our days are
almost broken, and the time will come when we won't have
our own government at all. But now we have to do the best
we can to keep what we have."

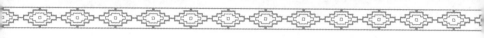

Jim did not often talk of these things to Tom, and Tom knew that he did so now because they were in the Choctaw capital. Tom had heard Choctaws before talk about "broken days." There was something about the sound of the words that made him feel a little sad.

But now they had reached the center of town and were caught up in the excitement of Council meeting time. Crowds of people, dressed in their best clothes, pushed along the street. A line of men stood outside the barber shop, waiting their turn. Women jammed the general stores buying cloth and household goods. Near one of the stores a tent was set up, and there were twenty or thirty people around it. When he and Jim passed it, Tom saw a sign that said:

⊷JEREMIAH STONE⊷
WORLD FAMOUS PHOTOGRAPHER
25¢ the Picture

"Jim," Tom said, "do you think we could get our picture taken together?"

"Sure," Jim said, "we'll do it while we're here."

They came to a three-story red brick building with a white peaked roof. It was well kept and the best building Tom had seen in the Territory. "That's the Choctaw capitol," Jim said.

They stopped to look at it, and as they stood there Tom saw a man pass in front of one of the second-story windows. He paused for a moment to look out over the crowded street, and Tom got a good look at him. He wore a black business suit, and his white hair contrasted almost startlingly with his brown Choctaw face. It was a strong, serious face; and as the man stood looking down at the people below, Tom felt sure somehow that this was Jonathan Wolf, Principal Chief of the Choctaws.

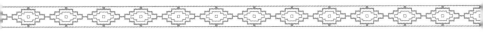

Tom touched Jim's arm and pointed to the window. "Is that Chief Wolf?" he asked.

Jim looked up at the window. "Yes," he said, a note of surprise in his voice, "it is. How did you know?"

"I don't know," Tom said. "Except he just looks like he's thinking about all the people down here."

"Yes," Jim said again, "I guess he is. The principal chief has a lot to think and worry about these days."

Tom would have liked to talk to Chief Wolf right then, but he couldn't think of any excuse to make to Jim. They went on down the street and at the Tuskahoma Hotel met Isom Kincade going in for lunch.

"Did you get our three friends taken care of?" Jim asked.

Kincade nodded. "As best we could," he said. "Iskitima will be tried next week. Welty and Bragg are being taken out of the Territory, but they'll probably come right back again."

"We can't try United States citizens in our courts," Jim explained to Tom. "We can turn a non-Choctaw lawbreaker over to the U.S. marshal, but if it's for something like whiskey running, they probably won't even be brought to trial."

They had lunch with Isom Kincade, had their picture taken in the afternoon by Jeremiah Stone, and about five o'clock went back to their horses.

"We'll ride to Nanih Waya and spend the night there," Jim said.

"Where is that?" Tom asked as he swung onto his horse.

"It's about two miles from here," Jim said. "It was the first capitol built after the Choctaws moved from the East."

They rode north out of Tuskahoma, staying in the valley, and came quickly to a good-sized Choctaw encampment.

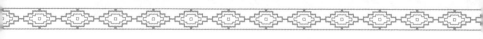

They were families mostly, and they were spread in a loose circle around the ruins of a great log building. Only parts of the walls were standing now, but Tom could hardly believe his eyes at the size of the mighty pine logs that had been used in the building.

"Some of the old people here tonight watched Nanih Waya being built when they were children," Jim said. "They came over the Trail of Tears with their parents."

Tom had learned enough Choctaw history to know about the Trail of Tears. Over fifty years ago, the Choctaws had been forced to leave their homes in Mississippi River. The move had been a terrible thing, with cholera and starvation killing hundreds of Choctaws. Hundreds of others lost everything they owned to robbers and dishonest men who were in charge of moving the Indians. The Choctaws had been promised that the new land would be theirs "as long as the grass shall grow and the waters shall run." Those were the very words of the removal treaty.

The Choctaws had gone to work and built new homes and set up a new government in this strange land. Now once again, just as it had happened many years ago, the white men were pressing in on them from all sides—from Arkansas, Texas, Kansas, and Missouri—and demanding the right to come in and work, start businesses, and even buy land. And every year more and more of them were coming in.

"What does Nanih Waya mean, Jim?" Tom asked as they hobbled their horses for grazing.

"You'll find out tonight when stories are told around the campfires," Jim said.

They were invited to eat with one of the families camped in the very shadow of Nanih Waya's walls. It was a large family made up of an old and wrinkled man, two of his sons, their wives, and eight small children. They ate roasted meat and abunaha, and for dessert had something that Tom had

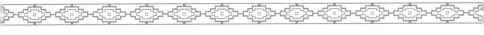

not eaten before. It was called *bahar* and was served in horn spoons. Tom thought it was pretty good, and Jim said that it was the food that Choctaws like above all others. It was made of hickory nuts, walnuts, cracked parched corn, and sugar. They were all mashed together and mixed with water until it became a sticky, doughy mass. The Choctaw children all wanted second helpings, but one was enough for Tom.

By the time they finished eating, it was dark. An old man stood up, raised a thin stick in the air, and snapped it with his fingers. Tom knew that the Choctaws marked the time before an event by breaking a stick for each day. This meant that the last day had been "broken." It was time to begin. Young men built up the fire, and then the old man began to talk in gutteral Choctaw. The children crept closer to him, but Jim and Tom moved back a little so that Jim could whisper to Tom what the old man was saying.

"He is telling them about how the Choctaw people began," Jim said softly. "A very long time ago, the whole earth was a bog, just a flat muddy field. One day a Great Red Man came down from his home in the sky, and he built a mound as high as a mountain in the middle of this muddy bog. He worked hard on the mountain and made trees and grass and flowers and cold, swift rivers. He filled the rivers with fish and the forests with animals whose flesh was good to eat and whose fur was warm. He made birds fly overhead; he made some of them to sing and others to be eaten. When he had finished his work, he named this great mound Nanih Waya, which means the mountain producer' or 'the mountain mother.'

"Then the Great Red Man decided to put people on Nanih Waya, and he could do this because he was all-powerful. He called forth Red People from the midst of the mountain, and these were the first Choctaws. The Great Red Man called the people together and laid down for them the laws they must obey, and he instructed them in how to live. He taught

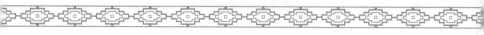

them that they must not kill one another or steal from one another. He taught them that they must not kill more animals or catch more fish than they needed to keep them from hunger. He taught them many more things that they must do to live happily together on the great mountain. The Red People lived together in peace and they learned to love the beautiful mountain, Nanih Waya, as a mother because they had come forth from it."

Jim paused to listen to the old Choctaw for a few minutes, and then he spoke again. "He is telling now of how the Choctaws, many hundreds of years ago, decided to move from their home, which was in the far west near where the sun sets. They traveled for many years, crossing high cold mountains and moving through deep forests and over vast, grass-covered prairies. At last they crossed the greatest river they had ever seen, and on the other side was a beautiful land where they decided to build their new nation. On their long journey they had carried with them the bones of all of the Choctaws who had died in their old home. They put these bones in one place, and they built a great mound of dirt over them. They called this mound Nanih Waya in memory of the beautiful mountain in their old home, the mountain that had been mother of all Choctaws. The chief of the Choctaws climbed to the top of the new mound and proclaimed again to the people the laws that had first been told to them by the Great Red Man. The people lived around the new Nanih Waya and were happy."

Later, when the fire had died down to a bed of glowing coals and everyone had settled down for the night, Tom shifted in his blankets and said to Jim, "I know those were mostly just stories tonight, but I kind of got the feeling that some of those things really happened."

"Yes," Jim said, "they were tribal legends, but I think you're right; there is probably a lot of truth in the legends. I

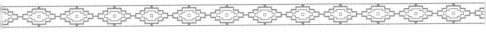

imagine the Choctaws did come to Mississippi from the far west a long time ago. And it's a fact that there was a mound called Nanih Waya in Mississippi. The Choctaws loved the land around Nanih Waya and really believed that the bones of their ancestors were buried there. Leaving the mound was one of the main reasons so many Choctaws fought against the Treaty of Dancing Rabbit Creek."

"That was the treaty that had the Choctaws give up their Mississippi land for this country, wasn't it?" Tom asked.

"That's right," Jim said, "and one of the first things the Choctaws did after they got here was build this big building for their first capitol, and they named it Nanih Waya to remind them of their old home."

"How come they let the building fall apart this way?" Tom asked, motioning in the dark to the ruined walls of Nanih Waya.

"About 1850 the location of the capital got into politics," Jim said, "and it moved around to places like Doaksville and Boggy Depot. But the main reason Tuskahoma is the capital now is because it is so close to Nanih Waya. Even if it is just a piece of a building, it means a lot to the older Choctaws, just because of the name."

Tom went to sleep feeling that he was getting more and more to know what it meant to Jim to be a Choctaw Indian.

CHAPTER 9

When Jim and Tom rode into Tuskahoma the next morning, a good-sized crowd was already in town. While they were stabling their horses, they met Isom Kincade, who went along with them.

"I'm going to talk for a couple of minutes to the General Council this morning, Tom," Jim said. "You can come along and sit in the gallery if you want, or poke around town if you'd rather."

"I'll come along," Tom said. He liked the idea of watching Jim talk to the Choctaw lawmakers.

"The big Choctaw ball play comes after the Council meeting today," Isom Kincade said to Tom as they walked along, "and Jim and I are on the same team. Do you think we're going to win?"

Tom looked at his two friends—Kincade, tall, lean, and strong; Jim, hard and powerful through the shoulders—and he said confidently, "I know you'll win." He was excited by the idea of seeing his first Choctaw ball game, but he realized that to Jim the meeting was more important.

They reached the red brick capitol and climbed the stairs to the General Assembly room. Jim took a seat near the front, and Tom and Kincade took a seat with the spectators at the back of the room. The meeting was already in session, but Tom couldn't make anything out of it because it was all in

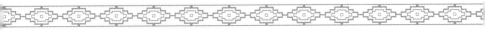

Choctaw. He saw Chief Jonathan Wolf sitting a little apart from the Council members, listening and making a note now and then.

"Can anybody talk before the Council?" Tom asked.

"No," Kincade said softly. "Jim was invited by some of the Council members, and it was approved by the Chief."

After a while Jim was called; and when he stood up, some of the people in the room clapped and even called out, but others were silent. Jim stood there looking calm and sure, but Tom's heart was beating rapidly. He knew that Jim would do well, but he was still half afraid that something would go wrong. Then Jim began to speak in Choctaw, and Isom Kincade leaned close to Tom and softly translated the words into English. This is what Jim said:

I am a Choctaw. I was born a Choctaw, and soon I will die a Choctaw. But while I live, it is important to me what happens to the Choctaw people. They are my people, and this is what I know about them: The Choctaws like to stay to themselves, but they are friendly and let other people come in. Choctaws love their country, but they do not pay enough attention to the bad things that a few people do to gain money and power. Choctaws think deep and are wise in many ways, but they are sometimes too trusting, and they do not know the ways of clever, land-hungry men. Choctaws are a religious people, but they can be violent in action. Do I not stand before you as an example of that? I do not want the time to come when Choctaws will rise up in hopeless bloodshed as they lose their land, piece by piece, to clever land buyers. You know me. You know that what I want is for the Choctaws to keep the good things that they have—their honor, their loyalty to each other, and their land. As long as the land is owned by the tribe, every man will always have as much as he needs, and a man with land is a free man. But if the land

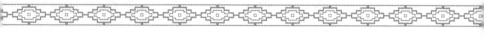

is divided up so that each Choctaw can do whatever he wishes with his little piece, the time will come when our sons' sons have no land. Whatever you decide to do cannot hurt me or help me. But as a Choctaw, I ask you not to hurt my friends who will go on living. A tribe is not a tribe without its land. Do not kill my tribe by giving away its land. Do not do that.

Jim sat down quickly. His speech had not taken more than three minutes, and no one seemed to be ready for it to end. There was complete silence in the Council room for several seconds, and then slowly a roar rose from both the Council and the gallery, and many people crowded forward to shake Jim's hand and talk to him. The chairman banged his fist on the table to restore order, but no one paid any attention. But again Tom noticed that some of the people did not seem to approve. They did not cheer or move from their seats.

During the height of the confusion, Tom saw Chief Jonathan Wolf stand and slowly leave the room. His face looked grave and thoughtful. Tom turned to Kincade and said, "I'm going out for a while, Isom. I'll find you and Jim later."

He moved away before Kincade could ask him where he was going. Outside the Council room, Tom saw Chief Wolf at the other end of the hall, turning into his office. Tom went quickly down the hall and knocked on the office door before he had a chance to think about it and lose his nerve. He knew that he would never have a better chance than this to talk to the Chief about Jim.

The door opened and the white-haired Chief stood there looking down at Tom.

"Please, Chief Wolf," Tom said, "may I come in and talk to you for a few minutes?"

A slow smile broke the seriousness of the Chief's face. "Of course," he said. "Come in."

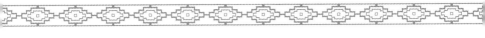

He closed the door behind Tom, motioned him to a seat, and sat down behind his desk. "I don't believe I know your name, young man," he said.

"It's Tom Baxter, sir," Tom said. "I've come to Tuskahoma with Jim Moshulatubbee."

The Chief looked surprised. "Oh," he said, "Jim usually travels alone."

"Jim and I are good friends," Tom said proudly. "He's been teaching me all about the forests and everything in them."

"You're lucky, Tom," Chief Wolf said. "You couldn't find a better teacher in the Choctaw Nation."

Tom was silent for a moment and then he said, "Chief Wolf, Isom Kincade told me that you were a powerful man and that if something that was wrong was going to happen, you could stop it."

Again the Chief smiled. "Not everyone would agree with Isom about that," he said. "But what is this wrong something that seems to be on your mind?"

"It's about Jim, sir," Tom said. "It's wrong that he is going to die for something he didn't intend to do."

The smile left the Chief's face. He rose from his desk and walked over to the window. "Does Jim know you're here, Tom?" he asked.

Now Tom was surprised. "No, sir," he said. "And he would be mad as anything if he knew I was here talking about him."

"Yes, of course," Chief Wolf said. "I'm sorry for even asking that question."

"Can you do something for Jim, Chief Wolf?" Tom asked.

The Chief bowed his head slightly. "Tom," he said, "even if I could, Jim wouldn't let me. Sentence was passed on him

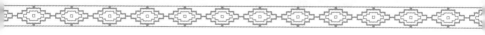

by a Choctaw court, and he wouldn't want anyone—not even me—to step in and make things easier for him."

"But it's not right," Tom said, feeling his throat beginning to tighten up a little. "Jim didn't mean to kill that man. Jim is a good man. You know it, and everybody knows it."

"Yes," Chief Wolf said, "Jim is a good man. I know it and probably most people who know him know it. But the fact is that he killed a man in anger, Tom. Perhaps he didn't intend to do it, but there's no way to prove that. No matter how good a reason he had, he did start the fight."

"But it's not right," Tom said again, because he wasn't able to say anything else. "It's not right."

Chief Wolf looked out the window for a moment and then turned back to Tom. "It's the Choctaw law, Tom," he said. "You say that you're Jim's friend. If that is true, then you know that Jim would be the last person to want the law interfered with to make things easier on him. You know how important honor is to him. He would never get over the shame of having his punishment made easier than the Choctaw court thought it should have been. It's been decided. Jim thinks it's right. That's what's important, Tom. I can't interfere."

The Chief walked over and put a hand on Tom's shoulder. "Jim is lucky to have a good friend like you at this time," he said. "But you will be the best kind of friend if you don't worry about this business anymore and instead help Jim enjoy his forests and his animals in the remaining time that he has. Believe me, that is the way Jim wants it. The days will be broken to the last. Then Jim will go—bravely."

Tom was silent for a moment. Talking to the Chief had helped. He saw things a little more clearly than he had before. Still, he hadn't helped Jim, and that gnawing feeling was there in his stomach, just the way it had been when he came in. But he realized the Chief had said all he could say.

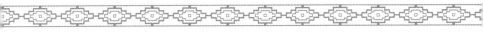

"All right, sir," Tom said. "I'll try to follow your advice."
He turned away, and then asked, "How many days are left
for Jim? How many unbroken?"

The Chief said, "Jim keeps his own pile of sticks and
breaks them as the days pass. I don't know for sure. I think
only a few are left now."

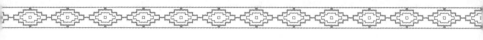

CHAPTER 10

Chief Wolf stood there for a long moment with his hand on Tom's shoulder, and then his mood changed abruptly. He looked at his pocket watch and said, "The big ball game is going to start in a few minutes. Why don't you come along with me, and we'll watch it together?"

"All right," Tom said, pleased with the idea of going to the game with the principal chief, and then he remembered his manners and added, "Thank you, Chief Wolf."

They left the office, and as they started down the stairs, Tom saw Isom Kincade coming out of the Council room. Tom waved and Kincade's mouth opened in surprise when he saw that Tom was with Chief Jonathan Wolf. He followed them to the head of the stairs and watched them as they climbed into the Chief's buggy and drove off.

"Have you watched a Choctaw ball game before?" the Chief asked as they drove along the main street.

Tom noticed that everyone stopped to look at them as they passed. "No, sir," he said, "I've just heard about it."

"It's the favorite Choctaw sport," Chief Wolf said. "We have played the same game for more than a hundred years."

The playing field was at the edge of town. When they arrived, it was already encircled with wagons and buggies full of people, and hundreds more stood or sat on the ground. A

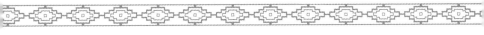

space in the best midfield location was left empty, and Chief Wolf drove his buggy into that.

"This is the big moment of Council-meeting time for many people," the Chief explained. "The best ballplayers from the whole Choctaw Nation come for this game. The teams are picked to make them as evenly matched as possible."

"I don't see how that could be," Tom said, "with Jim and Isom Kincade on the same team."

"You'll see," the Chief said with a smile.

The field, Tom judged, was about one hundred and fifty yards long, and maybe seventy-five wide. At each end was a tall, thick pole, but there were no lines or markings on the field. Tom turned to the Chief to ask when the teams would arrive, but before he could speak, a great shout rose up and the first players ran onto the field.

Tom stared, popeyed at the sight. Here were Indians like he had always imagined. The men running onto the field were dressed in nothing but breech cloths, and their copper-colored bodies seemed to shine in the sun. Each player had the tail of an animal tied to the back of his breech cloth, and the Chief explained that a player was supposed to represent the kind of animal whose tail he wore.

It took Tom a couple of minutes to spot Jim and Isom. When he did, he saw that Jim wore the tail of a badger and Isom that of a wolf. They looked strong and fast and hard, and Tom doubted again that the other team would have a chance.

And then he looked at the men running to the other end of the field, and he saw one man who made him forget all the others for a moment. The man was not especially big, but his body was beautifully built and his muscles were so smooth that they reminded Tom of a calmly flowing stream. All his movements were so effortless that they made Tom think of

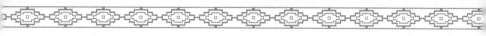

wind softly stirring the tops of pine trees. The man wore the tail of a panther.

"Who is that man?" Tom asked.

He didn't point or describe him, but Chief Wolf seemed to know whom he meant. "Many years ago," he said, "before my people moved from Mississippi, there was a great Choctaw ballplayer so skilled that no one man could match him. In fact, it is said that not even the second and third best players in the country teaming together against him were really a match for him. His name was Tullock-chisk-ko, which means 'He-Who-Drinks-the-Juice-of-the-Stone.' According to the stories told among the Choctaws, he never once in his life played on a team that lost."

Chief Jonathan Wolf pointed to the man wearing the panther tail. "He is the great-grandson of Tullock-chisk-ko, and he has taken that name for himself also. He is the reason why Jim Moshulatubbee and Isom Kincade must play on the same team."

The teams now gathered in two circles at each end of the field, and into each circle came an old Choctaw man dressed in buckskins and a blanket. The old men shouted something that sounded to Tom like "Hooklay, hook." Every time they shouted that, the players would shout back, "Hook!" They kept this up for a while, and then they all gave a great whoop, clapping their hands back and forth over their mouths.

At this point the old men led the teams in a dancing circle around the poles, and the players struck the poles with the sticks that each one carried. The sticks looked like small hickory saplings to Tom, and they had a kind of cup on the end. The players continued to give their yell as they went around the poles.

"That is called the *shookahfa*, Tom," the Chief explained. "The old men are supposed to be witches or medicine men, and the ritual is supposed to bring the team luck. No one

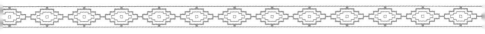

believes it much any more, but it is still a part of the fun of the game."

When the shookahfa ended, the teams lined up on the field and the game began. A small, round, skin-covered ball was put in play. It was a very simple game, and Tom understood it right away. Some of the team members were goal defenders and some were forwards who tried to move the ball down the field toward the pole of the enemy team. Chief Wolf explained that every time a team hit the other team's pole with the ball, they scored a point.

Jim and Isom played forwards and so did Tullock-chisk-ko. The first time Tullock-chisk-ko got the ball, Jim and Isom closed in quickly on him. But the great player passed the ball off easily to a team member, slipped effortlessly around Jim and Isom, and caught the ball on a return pass. Then with his stick he moved it down the field so swiftly that he ran away from both the opposing forwards and his own team members. The goal defenders rushed out to stop him; but just as the first one was almost on him, he caught the ball in the cupped end of his stick and hurled it at the pole. It sailed high over the heads of the goal defenders and thudded solidly against the pole. Tullock-chisk-ko's team had scored the first point.

On the next try, Jim and Isom brought the ball down the field, passing it between them. But on one pass, when it looked as if no player was close enough to cause trouble, Tullock-chisk-ko suddenly moved in with a great burst of speed, intercepted the ball, and raced away downfield with it. When all of the goal defenders moved in on him, he passed off to one of his teammates, who scored easily.

The game became very rough, and the crowd shouted encouragement to their favorite team. Tom had never seen Choctaw people show their feelings so much. The pace of the game speeded up even more, and sometimes a man was hurt

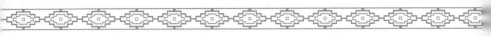

as he was blocked or shoved to the ground. But there were no fights, and there was no hitting with sticks. That was against the rules and could cause a team to lose points.

The game continued for a long time, and the sweaty bodies of the players glistened like polished copper in the bright sun. Jim and Isom began working smoothly together and scored several points, but no one could stop Tullock-chisk-ko for long at a time. Steadily his team pulled ahead, and when the game ended, Jim and Isom's team was thoroughly beaten.

"How can a man be that good?" Tom asked wonderingly as the teams ran from the field. "Half the players out there were bigger and stronger than Tullock-chisk-ko."

"But not one of them wanted to be a good player as much as Tullock-chisk-ko did," Chief Wolf said.

Tom looked at the Chief and said, "What you want and what happens aren't always the same thing."

"That is true," Jonathan Wolf said. He started to say something else but stopped and then repeated, "That is true." He picked up the buggy reins. "Do you want to ride back to town with me, Tom?"

"I'll wait here for Jim," Tom said. "Thank you, Chief Wolf. Sorry I troubled you."

"Tom," the Chief said, "I am troubled. But you didn't do it."

Jim and Isom came out of the forest soon, riding their horses and leading Tom's. Both men looked fresh and clean, and their hair glistened with water.

Isom grinned. "I didn't think you'd wait for us after we lost, especially when you had a chance to ride with the principal chief."

"Even Tom wouldn't expect us to best a panther," said Jim.

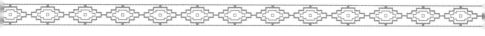

Jim didn't ask Tom how he happened to be with Chief Wolf, and Tom appreciated that. It would have been hard to explain.

In town the main street was crowded with people talking loudly about the game. Jim, Isom, and Tom tied their horses to a hitching rail and joined in the excitement. But suddenly Jim was confronted by a slight, thin-faced man with long, carefully trimmed sideburns and a small, neat mustache. He wore an expensive-looking black suit, and a diamond stickpin glittered in his wide black tie. Tom guessed from his looks that he was half Choctaw, half white.

"It's Jim Moshulatubbee, the great Choctaw orator," the man said, and Tom thought he heard a little slur in the man's words, as if he had been drinking. "That was a wonderful speech you made this morning, Jim. I'm sure it brought tears to every Standpatter eye in the assembly hall."

"I said what I felt, Roger," Jim said.

A humorless smile played on the thin man's lips. "How much were you paid by the Standpatters to feel that way?"

A muscle twitched in Jim's jaw, but he said quietly, "What would I need money for?"

"To run out of the country. That's what you need it for," the man named Roger said. "You talk big now about standing up to a bullet, but when the time comes, you'll be long gone. Then we'll see what people think of your wonderful Standpatter traditions, honor, and loyalty."

"There isn't anything to do but wait and see, is there?" Jim said, stepping around the thin man and moving on down the street.

The man stared hatefully at Jim's back, and Tom said to Isom as they walked on to catch up with Jim, "Who is that man?"

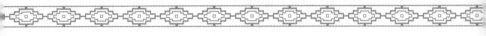

"His name is Roger Going," Isom said. "He is lawyer for the Progressives, besides being the chief member of the party."

"Do you think he really believes what he was saying to Jim?" Tom asked.

"I wouldn't know," Isom said. "He sounded like he believed it."

"Well, he's crazy if he thinks Jim will run," Tom said.

And then Tom stopped short, and his own words seemed to ring in his ears. He himself had tried to get Jim to run. He had hoped he would run. And now he was saying to Isom that a person was crazy to think that Jim would run!

"He won't run," Isom said softly. "Jim won't run. He's real Choctaw."

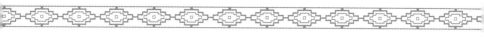

CHAPTER 11

On the way back from Tuskahoma Jim and Tom attended a pashofa dance. Tom had heard about these dances that were held for sick people, but he had never seen one before. They had ridden by to see another of Jim's friends and had found the cabin clearing full of people. A black and white striped pole was stuck in the ground near the cabin door.

"Hopia is sick," Jim said as they dismounted. "His friends are holding a pashofa dance to help him get well."

Jim talked to an old Choctaw woman for a moment and said to Tom, "Hopia has a fever. He lives alone, so no one found out about it for a long time. The medicine man is inside with him now. No one else is allowed inside."

"What is the pole for?" Tom asked.

"It marks the spot which no one can go past while the medicine man is with the sick person. If anyone goes past it, Shulop, the spirit of disease, will get into him. But the people are supposed to dance to help the medicine man drive Shulop out of the sick person."

At that moment a loud chant came from inside the cabin. The men and women outside the cabin repeated the chant and then began to dance. The chant of the medicine man continued, and the people danced wildly in circles and other patterns. All the time they continued to repeat the chant of

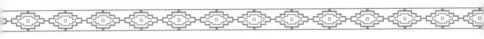

the medicine man. Jim sat apart with a few of the old people who were not dancing.

The dancing continued all morning at the same frenzied pace. At noon the dancers stopped, sat in a circle, and ate a great kettleful of pashofa that was passed around in horn spoons. When the whole huge kettle of pashofa was eaten, the chanting of the medicine man began again, and the dancing resumed.

Jim and Tom rode on then, and Jim said, "They'll keep dancing until they all drop from exhaustion."

"How come you didn't dance?" Tom asked.

"I don't believe it helps a sick person to get well," Jim said, "but I don't laugh at people who dance, the way some young Choctaws do. The old people think they're helping, and besides, it lets a sick person know he has friends. And that's a good thing."

"But your friend Hopia ought to have a doctor," Tom said.

Jim nodded. "I'll try to get a missionary doctor and ride back out this evening." They rode along silently for a while, and then Jim said, almost to himself, "People who still try to dance away spirits are no match for land-grabbers."

Again they rode on in silence. Then Jim turned in his saddle and said, "I kept you at that pashofa dance for a reason, Tom. I wanted you to see that part of Choctaws too. So maybe you'll understand better."

"Understand what?" Tom asked.

"Lots of things. We have people like Roger, for instance. They are educated in the best schools of the East and are full of learning and law. We have the kind you saw dancing themselves foolish outside Hopia's cabin. And we have people like me. I don't belong to either. I know that the people at the cabin are good. I know that people like Roger are smart. But

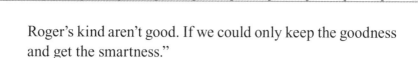

Roger's kind aren't good. If we could only keep the goodness and get the smartness."

They reached Atoka late in the afternoon. Tom had enjoyed Tuskahoma, but it was still good to get home to see his folks and catch up on his mother's cooking. He spent the next few days mostly around the house, doing the yard work and telling his parents all about the trip to the Choctaw capital. He told them with a touch of special pride how he and Jim had caught the whiskey runners.

So much had been happening that he was surprised when his mother reminded him a few days later that his birthday was coming up in a week's time. He had forgotten all about it, which was something that had never happened before.

"Why don't you ask Jim to come in?" Tom's mother said. "I'll fix a special meal and have birthday cake and ice cream."

"Swell," Tom said and went out to tell Jim that very day.

During the next week Tom spent quite a bit of time in the forest with Jim. They did about the same things as usual—fishing, swimming, and just walking. They spent some time looking for a honey tree that Jim thought was somewhere near the boulders where they had caught the copperhead, but they didn't find the tree.

Tom noticed that Jim was quieter than usual. And he seemed to take an extra long look at some things, as if he was not going to see them again for a long time. Tom didn't know when Jim's execution day was, but he knew it couldn't be far off now; and it seemed to Tom that Jim was going around to his favorite places and saying goodbye to them one by one.

Tom's birthday came on Sunday. After they got home from church, his parents gave him their present: a big silver railroad watch, just like his dad's, with his name and the date engraved on the back. And there was a solid silver chain

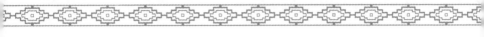

fastened to it. Tom was as proud of the watch as anything he had ever owned, and he could hardly wait to show it to Jim.

At one o'clock Hannah Baxter had the birthday dinner ready, but Jim hadn't come. "Are you sure you told him the right day, Tom?" she asked.

"Sure, I'm sure," Tom said. "I wouldn't tell him the wrong date of my own birthday."

"It's not like Jim to forget," Harvey Baxter said.

"I'm sure he wouldn't," Tom's mother said. "You know I told you that he came to see me about a present for Tom."

"What kind of present?" Tom asked.

His mother smiled. "You'd better wait until Jim comes. Then you'll see."

But at one thirty Jim still wasn't there, and Hannah said that they would have to eat or the roast wouldn't be any good. It was a fine meal, and Tom thought that the ice cream and cake were the best his mother had ever made. But everyone was wondering about Jim, and no one ate as much as they usually did for a birthday dinner. As soon as the meal was over, Tom slid out of his chair.

"I'm going to go see about Jim," he said.

Tom went straight to Jim's cabin, and it was open as it always was, but Jim wasn't there. Tom waited for a while and then went to a few places in the forest where he thought Jim might be. But there wasn't any sign of him, and when Tom called his name, there was nothing but silence.

Tom went back to the cabin, and Mr. Bronson, the Indian agent, was there. "You looking for Jim too?" he asked Tom. "Thought I'd come out and chat with him, but he doesn't seem to be around here any place."

"He's bound to be back soon," Tom said.

"I don't know," Mr. Bronson said doubtfully. "Both his horses are gone."

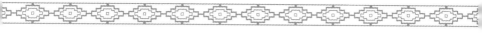

Tom looked around and saw that Mr. Bronson was right. He had been so busy looking for Jim that he hadn't even noticed about the horses. Tom couldn't remember when Jim had ever gone off with both horses.

Tom and Mr. Bronson waited around for a while longer and then walked back to town together. They didn't talk much, but as Tom turned up the path to his house, Mr. Bronson said, "Wouldn't surprise me if Jim has sneaked out of the country. His time is up in just a few days."

Tom hadn't even thought about that. He knew that Jim hadn't sneaked away. It made him mad for Mr. Bronson to even say it. "Jim wouldn't do that," Tom said.

His voice carried his anger, and Mr. Bronson looked at him in surprise. "Oh," he said, "you think so, do you, young fellow?"

"Yes," Tom said. "Jim said he was coming to my birthday dinner today, and if he had intended not to come, he'd have told me."

"Well, did he come?"

"No," Tom said, "but there must have been something that kept him from coming."

"I imagine there was," Mr. Bronson said. "It's probably because he's on his way to Texas." Mr. Bronson walked away looking pleased with himself.

Tom shouted after him. "Jim wouldn't run away. He just wouldn't run—ever!"

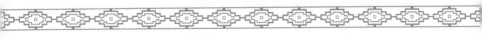

CHAPTER 12

Tom went into the house and found his mother and father in the living room. "1 couldn't find him," he said. "And the funny thing is that both his horses are gone."

Tom saw his parents look at each other. "That is odd," his father said. "I suppose we might as well tell you, Tom. Jim planned to give you the horse you rode to Tuskahoma as a birthday present."

Tom's heart jumped. "The buckskin!" he said.

"Well," Hannah Baxter said, "I just don't understand this at all. Jim simply isn't the kind of man to say he was bringing the horse for Tom and then not do it."

"It's a puzzler, all right," Mr. Baxter said. "But maybe he had to make a trip and rode one horse and took the other one for supplies."

"He still would have told us he was going," Tom said, and he could tell from his father's face that he agreed.

Early the next morning Tom went back to Jim's cabin, but he wasn't there. The bed didn't show any signs of having been slept in, and there wasn't any smell of cooked food in the room. Jim's rifle was not on its wall pegs, but that didn't mean anything. He always took it with him no matter where he went. It was just like a part of him.

Tom searched the woods all morning and called. The woods were silent. All the while Tom kept thinking that things had taken a strange twist. Until yesterday he had half-way hoped that Jim would run away. But now that he was gone, Tom found himself hoping that Jim hadn't run away. He didn't want him to be shamed in the eyes of his people. And he didn't want people like Mr. Bronson to smile and say, "That's what an Indian's honor is worth."

Tom didn't believe that Jim had run. Jim wouldn't run. Jim had said that it would be wrong to run.

When Tom came back to the cabin, he saw Mr. Bronson there. Tom circled around the cabin and went on home. He didn't want to see the Indian agent then. He and his wife had been against Jim from the start.

That afternoon word started getting around town that Jim had left the country. Tom heard the white people talking about it on the streets. He saw the Indians sitting around, not saying anything. Worst of all, Roger Going, the lawyer who had belittled Jim in Tuskahoma, happened to be in Atoka, and he was the first one to start spreading the word that Jim had run away. It was plain that Going intended to use Jim's absence to hurt the Standpatter Choctaws and help the Progressives.

Billy Wakaya, the Choctaw high sheriff, was not out looking for Jim. He sat in his office, quietly. There wasn't any question of the sheriff's trying to find Jim and bring him back. If Jim wanted to run, nobody would stop him; and so Billy Wakaya sat in his office with his hands folded and his face expressionless and looked toward the hills. He talked to no one and listened to no one. Billy was an old friend of Jim's.

Late that afternoon Tom couldn't eat any supper, and his mother was upset. "Tom," she said, "you mustn't carry on this way. If Jim has gone, I think it's a good thing. It just isn't right to give a man his freedom and then expect him to

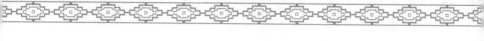

wait around for his own execution. If he's gone, then good for him."

"But he wouldn't think it was good," Tom said. "That's why I know he hasn't run away. And if he hasn't, where is he?"

Hannah Baxter sounded worried. "To tell the truth, I don't think he has run either. I just keep telling myself he has, because I'd like to think he's all right."

Harvey Baxter had been sitting in his easy chair, staring at the *Indian Citizen*, without turning the pages. He put the newspaper aside and said, "Tom, there aren't any trains tomorrow. Maybe we'd best go out into the woods and look around some."

It made Tom feel good to know that his mother and father were on Jim's side. "I'll be ready at sunup," he said. "Thanks, Dad."

"He's my friend too," Harvey Baxter said. "No need to thank me."

The next morning Tom and his father started out early. Before he left his bedroom, Harvey Baxter strapped on his army pistol. "Probably won't need it," he said. "But won't do any harm to tote it. We might see some game out there."

They checked at Jim's cabin first. It was empty and looked just the way Tom had seen it the day before. Not a pan or a plate had been moved. "Well, Tom," Mr. Baxter said, "you lead the way into the woods. You know the places Jim might be."

Tom headed for the hills where they had hunted the deer. They searched for more than three hours and then dropped down and spent two more hours checking spots along the Clear Boggy. They didn't find a thing, and Tom knew that his dad was getting pretty tired.

"Let's head back to Jim's cabin and fix something to eat," Tom said. "Then we can look some more."

Tom led his father in a straight line across the hills, and in half an hour's time they were on the ridge overlooking the miserable clapboard cabin that Tom had first seen on the day he met Jim. Tom knew that the Indian who had owned it had moved out of the country, but now a thin wisp of smoke came from the rusted crooked chimney.

Tom stared down at the cabin and said to his father, "You wait here and rest. I'm going down there for a minute."

He moved carefully and quietly down the ridge. Except for one spot, the clearing was overgrown with brush, and he was able to get almost to the cabin and still stay completely hidden. He didn't really know why he was taking such pains to stay out of sight and make no noise, but he did know that if someone were inside the cabin, it wasn't Jim. He remembered the look of disgust on Jim's face every time they passed this cabin.

There were no windows in the cabin, so Tom circled silently around to the single door, and he saw that it was ajar. He crept across the few yards of clear ground and edged down the cabin wall until he was pressed against the rough boards behind the door. It was half open.

For a moment he heard nothing and then someone whined. "Ain't that coffee ready yet?"

Tom felt the hair on his neck prickle. It was the voice of Pete Welty. He would recognize that whine anywhere. He crouched low and chanced a peek through the crack of the door below the sagging leather hinge. It was Welty. Tom could see enough of him slouched at the table. Standing in front of a rusted iron stove was the tall scarecrow figure of Hiram Bragg. And then Tom's eyes swept around the part of the room he could see, and his heart twisted and began to thump. In one corner stood two rifles. One was a .30-30 with

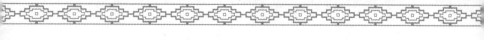

a finely polished oak stock and filed sights. He would have known the gun anywhere—it was Jim's.

He crept away from the door and ran low, below the brush line, all the way to the ridge. Even though they were far from the cabin, he still whispered a warning to his father. "Dad! They're down there. Hiram Bragg and Welty. And they've got Jim's gun standing in the corner."

Harvey Baxter moved to his feet, and his pistol was in his hand in one fast motion. "You sure, Tom?"

"I'd know that pair anywhere. And I could pick Jim's .30-30 out of a hundred other rifles. I'd best run for some help."

"That would take time," Harvey Baxter said. "They've got Jim's rifle. Do they have another?"

"Yes," Tom said. "But both guns are pretty far from where Welty and Bragg are."

Harvey Baxter looked thoughtful. It was the way Tom had always imagined his father looking before a battle, not scared, but not crazy brave either. "If I could bust in before they get to the rifles . . . Then again, if you could get to town and get Billy Wakaya, they'd never try to shoot it out with Billy. But they might get away if we don't move fast." Harvey Baxter grinned, and Tom's heart turned over. He knew that look. "I think I'd better go in on them," Harvey said. "You wait here. If anything happens, you run to town and get Billy Wakaya. Understand?"

"Yes," Tom said. "Be careful."

"I'm always that," Harvey Baxter said. "You may die of old age before I work my way up on them. But don't fret."

"Good luck," Tom whispered to his father, but by then Harvey Baxter had spun the cylinder of his pistol, checked the loading, and was moving off into the scrub.

His father worked low, and surprisingly little of his big bulk showed above the scrub. He moved in a wide circle, away from the open door and on the blind side of the cabin. Watching him, Tom lost some of his anxiety. His father might not be a hunter, but he was a soldier. Moving up on armed men was something he knew about. There was only the one bad spot where the ridge line dipped and there was no covering scrub. The bare spot was in a direct line with the half-open door. Watching his father move toward it, Tom began to bite down on his clenched fist. His father was awful big to cross a spot like that. Even Jim would have trouble making it. His father was almost up to the bare spot. Did his father realize from where he was how little cover there was? Tom wondered.

He did. His father had reached the bare spot and had stopped in the scrub. Nothing moved. His father must have been lying out flat, watching the doorway for any sign of movement in the cabin.

Tom waited. He kept checking the scrub, but nothing moved down there. What was his father doing? He had said it would take a while. But he wasn't even moving. Then Tom saw a bush move, ever so slightly. His father was stirring. But he could not see his father. Only the brush moved. One clump of brush was slowly separating from the rest and moving slowly out into the clear space. Watching it, Tom saw the sun hit on metal. His father was under that moving brush, carrying his pistol so that it showed up on the ridge but not to the cabin.

Move, like a great green bug, and then stop. Move a few inches and stop. That was how his father crossed the bare spot. Not once did he hurry. Not once did he try to make more than a few inches at a time. It was beautiful, Tom realized. He wished Jim could have seen it.

His father had gained the brush on the other side of the clear spot. For a while there was no movement there, and

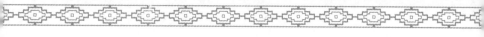

then Tom saw him, quite far down the slope and almost at the cabin wall.

He worked slowly along the blind wall of the cabin. Just behind the door he swung up his pistol and checked it again. His father was a very careful man. Then he stepped forward and kicked the door the rest of the way open and disappeared into the dark doorway of the cabin.

From the ridge Tom heard a yell which followed the enormous thunder of his father's big pistol. Then silence. Tom broke out of the brush and ran toward the house, yelling, "Pa! Pa!"

When he came into the cabin, Tom saw Hiram Bragg standing in the corner with his hands above his head. Pete Welty was on the floor.

"He fell right over his chair when I busted in," Harvey Baxter said. "There, Tom, on the floor, is a real tough outlaw. Get up, Welty. Hands high."

"Don't shoot, Baxter," Welty said. "I'm an unarmed man."

Harvey Baxter said, "Get over there and get your hands flat on that table. You too, Bragg. Go!"

Bragg and Welty slouched toward the table and spread their hands out. Harvey Baxter had pulled the rifles over near the door. He motioned to Tom to pick them up.

From the table, Bragg said: "You got no right busting in here. We ain't done nothin'."

"You got Jim Moshulatubbee's rifle," Harvey Baxter said. "Where'd you get it?"

"Who says it's his?" Welty demanded. "Lots of .30-30s out here."

"I say it's his," Tom said. "I'd know it anywhere."

"You should shut your mouth, kid," Bragg said. "Jest shut your mouth."

"I'll say who does that around here," Harvey Baxter said. "Now talk."

"We bought it," Welty said. "He sold it to us. He needed money to clear out of the country. We paid cash money for it."

"That's a lie," Tom said.

Harvey Baxter shook his head. "It's a lie, Tom, but all you'll get out of 'em is lies. We'd better take them in to Billy Wakaya."

Baxter waved the two men to their feet, and walking behind them, herded them up toward the ridge.

At the top of the ridge stood a man, casting a huge shadow down on to the trail. It was Gipson Bohanon, the bear hunter. When he saw him, Tom dashed ahead, "Gipson," he shouted. "Welty and Bragg may have bushwhacked Jim. They had his rifle. But they won't say where he is."

Bohanon moved forward, and Welty and Bragg tumbled back down the hill. "Don't give us to him," Welty begged. "He ain't even human!"

Bohanon moved forward. "Talk," the bear hunter commanded of Welty. "Talk!"

Harvey Baxter said, "It's better to take them in to Billy Wakaya. We don't know that they've done anything. I'll take them in. You and Tom start hunting. Jim can't be far."

"Yes," Bohanon said. "We go look for Jim's horses. They must be close."

Bohanon and Tom headed into the densest part of the brush, Bohanon moving with the quiet ease of a hunter, and Tom, after long practice, close and quiet behind him. Bohanon bent down. His sharp eyes had picked up a sign. A large animal had gone through the scrub oak thicket. He waved Tom on. The marks were too old to leave a clear trail and dark was coming on, but Bohanon kept moving.

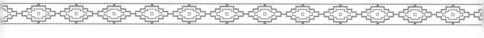

They came upon the horses, suddenly. The fine red roan and the little buckskin were inside a brush corral, hobbled. Welty and Bragg had taken no chances.

"There's no question now," Tom said. "Welty and Bragg lied."

"They lie," Bohanon agreed.

They drove the horses into town and brought them in front of Billy Wakaya's office. When he saw the horses, Wakaya went into the jail and herded out Welty and Bragg. "So Jim cleared out of the country, did he?" Wakaya yelled at the two terrified outlaws. "I guess he just left his horses for you to care for."

"We don't know nothin'," Welty whined. "Who sez we had those horses? You didn't find us with them."

Wakaya turned to a crowd that had begun to gather. "Now easy, boys. Welty is lying. No doubt of that. But the way to help Jim is to get out and look for him. I'm going to form up two parties. Gipson, you'll take one and search the high ground. I'll take the other. It's pretty dark for tracking, but we might get something done before dark. Jim might be hurt and have built a fire out there we could see." He turned to Tom. "You must be dead tired. And your pa too. Why don't you leave it to us until morning?"

"He's right, Tom," Harvey Baxter said, softly. "We'd be better off to go home and rest. Tomorrow we'll go out again."

"I won't sleep," Tom said. "I want to go out now."

Billy Wakaya said, "Tom, I know how you feel. He is my friend too. But I run this posse. And I say you need some rest. That's an order from the sheriff."

Tom let his father lead him away from the men. He was ashamed, but he said nothing in front of the others.

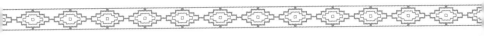

"We'll find him tomorrow," Harvey Baxter promised. "Wait and see."

As they walked into the darkness, Tom said, "If you don't mind, I'd like to sleep in Jim's cabin tonight. Just so we can get an early start."

"All right, son," Harvey Baxter said. "Anything you say. We can ride the horses back there and head out early."

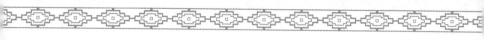

CHAPTER 13

Tom was awakened the next morning by the sound of a bee as it buzzed around his bed. He lay there listening to it, slowly remembering where he was and all that had happened yesterday; and suddenly he sat up straight. Just as surely as if he had seen him, he knew where Jim was.

"Pa!" he yelled.

Harvey Baxter raised up from the fireplace where he was cooking bacon. "Right here, Tom."

Tom said, "I know where Jim is."

Mr. Baxter brought the bacon over to the table. "What do you mean, Son?" he asked.

"I just know," Tom said. "One of the last times I was out with Jim, he was looking for a new honey tree. You know how Jim is. He never came to our house without bringing Mom something. I'll bet he was out looking for that honey tree so he could bring some when he came in for my birthday. And I'll bet that's where Welty and Bragg bushwhacked him."

"It's as good a guess as any," Tom's father said. "Do you know where this tree is?"

"I know where Jim was looking for it," Tom said.

They had a quick breakfast and set out on the horses for the boulder-strewn area. When they reached the boulders, they tethered their horses and began the search on foot. They

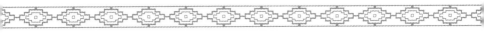

went into the forest on the far side of the rocks and looked for over an hour with no success. Then they found the honey tree, and they could tell that honey had been taken from it recently, but there was no trace of Jim anywhere around it.

Mr. Baxter sat down on a log and said, "Tom, we could go on like this for a month and not find Jim. We've got to try to think this out. Let's assume that Jim got the honey and started back to his cabin. Do you think you can pick the way he probably would have gone?"

Tom thought a minute. "I'm pretty sure I could," he said. "There's a trail about a quarter mile from here, and it leads pretty close to Jim's cabin. If he was carrying honey or riding his horse, he probably would have cut right over and followed the path."

Mr. Baxter nodded. "And Bragg and Welty probably would have been on a path. I can't see those two beating around out in the brush if they didn't have to. Let's look around first about where Jim would have come on to the path."

They cut directly over to the trail, and Mr. Baxter pointed to where it came down a ridge. "If Bragg and Welty had just happened to be coming down there, they could have seen Jim cutting through the brush for quite a distance before he got to the trail. They could have got down here and got set to ambush him."

They combed the area carefully, foot by foot, and it took a long time. They were about fifty feet off the trail in a spot where the brush was heaviest along a tiny stream. Tom was about ready to give up when, through an open space in a clump of thorn bush, he saw what looked like a piece of buckskin. Jim always wore a buckskin shirt.

They went around the thorn bush, and they found him.

He lay right at the edge of the stream, face down, with his head resting on one outstretched arm, as if he were sleeping.

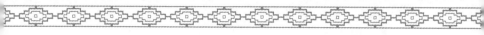

Mr. Baxter moved ahead of Tom and knelt down beside Jim. He crouched there for a moment, and then he said, "Tom, he's alive—barely. Go get the horses, quick!"

Tom moved through the forest as he never had before. He got the roan and the buckskin and was back in fifteen minutes. Together they got Jim onto the roan and secured him with a piece of rope that Mr. Baxter had brought along. Then they started the trip to town, getting the horses into a smooth, steady walk.

"You can't expect much, Tom," his father said. "Jim is hurt bad, shot through the back, and he's probably been lying there for three days. It looked like he had dragged himself to that stream, so maybe he's had a little water, but that's all. I've seen wounds, and he's hurt bad."

"I know," Tom said, and left it at that, because there was nothing else to say.

They reached the road to town and were riding past their house when Hannah Baxter came out to meet them. "Bring him in here, Harvey," she said, as if she had been expecting them.

"I thought I'd take him right to the doctor," Mr. Baxter said.

"You bring him in here," Mrs. Baxter said again, "and go for the doctor."

They got Jim into Tom's bed, and Tom himself rode the mile to where Dr. Seabring, the Baptist missionary doctor, lived. The doctor was at home, and he grabbed his bag and came right with Tom. At the Baxter house he took a quick look at Jim, called for hot water and clean white sheeting, and spread his instruments out.

"I may need your help, Mr. Baxter," Dr. Seabring said, and Tom and his mother went out of the room and closed the door.

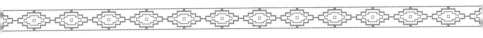

They waited in the living room for what seemed like a long time but was really only half an hour. Then the door of the bedroom opened, and both the doctor and Mr. Baxter came out.

"It doesn't look good," Dr. Seabring said. "The bullet passed clear through him and that's a blessing. But he's lost a lot of blood, and there's infection. I've done what I can for now. I'll be around again this evening."

Mrs. Baxter nodded and the doctor left the house. Mr. Baxter had to go to the train station, and Tom—suddenly with nothing to do—felt lost and empty and very, very tired. He lay down on the couch in the living room, and the weariness of three days' searching washed over him. He fell asleep instantly.

When Tom awoke, shadows were long in the room, and he heard his father and Dr. Seabring talking on the front porch. "I don't know what's keeping Jim alive," the doctor said. "An ordinary man never would have survived those days in the forest."

"Did you know that tomorrow was to have been his execution day?" Mr. Baxter asked.

"I know it," Dr. Seabring said. "That's one date that Jim Moshulatubbee won't keep."

It came to Tom as he lay there that he could tell Dr. Seabring what was keeping Jim alive. Maybe he wouldn't keep his date tomorrow, but he would keep it just as soon as he could. That was Jim's way; that was the Choctaw way. Jim was fighting to die the way he thought he should.

That night as they were finishing supper, Billy Wakaya came around. "I thought you'd like to know," he said, "that Welty and Bragg have confessed to shooting Jim. The U.S. Deputy Marshal has them now, and they're on their way to Fort Smith. They won't be fouling the Choctaw Territory any more."

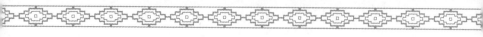

The sheriff opened the bedroom door slightly and looked in at Jim. "He doesn't look too good," he said doubtfully. "He looks real bad."

"He's alive, but he doesn't show any signs of regaining consciousness." Mrs. Baxter agreed.

"Billy," Mr. Baxter said, "suppose that Jim does live. Will this thing make any difference in his sentence?"

The sheriff rubbed his jaw. "I'm not a lawyer, Harvey, but I don't think so," he said, and added after a moment's thought, "But I sure hope he pulls through."

"Why?" Hannah Baxter asked bitterly. "So he can face another bullet?"

Billy Wakaya said, "I think Jim would like that better than going to his grave from a coward's bullet in the back. And I notice you're taking mighty good care of him, Hannah."

Tom made his bed at night now on the living room couch, but everyone in the Baxter family took turns sitting up with Jim throughout the night. Mrs. Baxter said that there should always be someone awake and beside his bed in case he regained consciousness in the night and wanted or needed something. Tom was sitting beside Jim when he first came out of his coma. It was about five o'clock in the morning, and Tom had just taken over the watch from his mother. He sat in the rocker near the foot of the bed, and his eyelids drooped because he was still full of sleep.

When he first heard the voice—it was only a whisper—he thought he had been dreaming. But then it came again, someone whispering his name. He opened his eyes and sat up in the chair. He looked up and looked right into Jim's eyes. A little smile was on Jim's lips.

"Hello, Tom," he said, still in a whisper. "You were a real woodsman to find me out there."

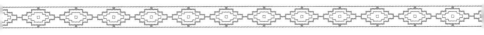

He closed his eyes again and seemed to be asleep. Tom jumped from the chair and ran to his parents' room. "Mom!" he said. "Jim is awake!"

His mother went quickly into Jim's room. Jim opened his eyes in greeting when she came in but closed them again as if the effort to keep them open was too great. Tom's mother bustled into the kitchen and made some hot chocolate and heated some meat soup. She took them back to Jim and insisted that he take a few sips of each before he went back to sleep.

When they left the room again with Jim asleep, Tom's mother looked up and smiled. "He'll come along now, I think," she said.

And he did, though it was still a slow thing. There were still times when Dr. Seabring said to Mr. Baxter, "I don't know what keeps him alive."

But Tom knew how Jim felt and thought. He understood how important it was for him to live like a Choctaw, and, if he must, to die like a Choctaw.

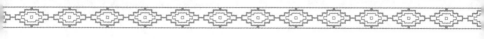

CHAPTER 14

The days passed slowly and turned into weeks. At first it was a greater effort than Jim could make to stay awake or sit up and try to eat the good food that Hannah Baxter brought him. But Hannah was a good nurse, and she made taking care of Jim her main job. She coaxed him at just the right times, scolded him gently when she thought he was not eating the way he should, and was always as patient and tireless as a human being could be. Tom and his father helped too, but the real job was done by Hannah. Jim responded steadily, and in two weeks he was sitting up in a chair for a little while each day. At the end of three weeks he could stand and even walk around the house a little.

Then he began to fret. "Hannah," he said, "it isn't right for me to double your work this way. I'm plenty well enough to leave now and rest up in my cabin."

But he wasn't and he knew it. When Hannah said, "Jim, if you talk like that again I'll have you tied down," he smiled and seemed satisfied.

Tom spent a part of every day talking to Jim about Choctaw history and customs and forest lore. He rode out to Jim's cabin almost every day to make sure that everything was all right, and he went fishing two or three times a week because Jim always seemed to have an appetite for a good bass or channel cat.

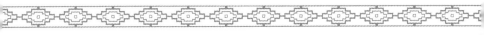

Just as soon as he had been able to talk, Jim had told Tom that the little buckskin was his. Tom made an old shed at the back of their lot into a fine stable, and he kept both the buckskin and the roan there. He named the buckskin Buff, and he rode him everywhere, even the little way downtown to do chores for his mother.

One day when Tom was in town, he came face to face with Roger Going, the Progressive leader and lawyer, as he walked along the board sidewalk.

"I hear that Jim Moshulatubbee is still at your house," Going said.

"That's right," Tom told him cautiously.

Going smiled humorlessly, and again Tom thought there was the smell of whiskey about him. Going said, "I hear, too, that he's trying to wiggle out of his sentence."

"You hear more than I do," Tom said and pushed around Going, just as Jim had done in Tuskahoma.

Tom said nothing about his meeting with the lawyer because he knew that it would only bother Jim. But that night Billy Wakaya came around to the Baxter house.

"Jim," the sheriff said, "some of your friends in town are talking it around that your sentence doesn't hold any more. They're saying that you were just the same as dead from Bragg and Welty's bullet and that that was just the same as the sentence being carried out. They say you should go a free man now."

"I hadn't heard anything about such talk," Jim said.

Wayaka said, "I didn't figure you had."

Jim was silent for a moment, and when he spoke, Tom thought he heard a note of hope in his voice. "And what does our law say about this, Billy?" he asked.

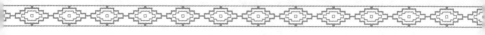

"Our law doesn't say anything, Jim," the sheriff told him. "It's just a lot of wishing your friends are doing. Nothing is changed. I checked with the judge on that."

Jim nodded. "Of course," he said. "Why are you telling me this, Billy?"

"Well," the sheriff said, "you know how stories grow and get around. You might have heard it from one of your friends as the real thing and got your hopes up."

Jim smiled. "It takes a real friend to come here and tell me not to. Thanks, Billy."

Once Jim was able to move around regularly, he began to regain weight and mend faster. He might have been able to move back to his cabin then, but he seemed to enjoy the company of the Baxters. Hannah sensed his desire to stay with them and insisted that he wasn't ready to move anywhere. So Jim stayed.

One day when Jim and Tom were in the stable looking over the horses, Jim turned to Tom and said, "Your mom is worn to a frazzle from taking care of me, Tom. She needs a vacation and a rest, and I aim to see that she gets one. I've got money saved from trapping last winter, and I want her to use it for a trip back to St. Louis. Of course, she can't go alone and your dad can't get away to go with her. So I'd like for you to go."

Tom had always known that this moment was going to come. He didn't know exactly what day it would be, but he knew that the time for Jim's sentence to be carried out was almost here. Jim wanted him to be out of town on that day, and so he had worked up this trip to St. Louis. Tom knew it was best for him to be gone on that day, and for his mother, too, for that matter. But still it did seem a little like running away.

"What day do you figure Mom will want to start?"

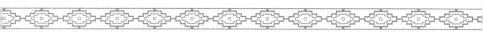

Jim said, "About this day next week, Tom. I've already talked to her."

The next day Tom and Jim went to the forest again for the first time since Jim had been shot. They rode their horses and moved at an easy pace, but in two days' time they visited all of their favorite spots. They spent the night at Jim's cabin and made a fresh batch of pashofa. Jim ate hungrily, because it was the first he had had in a long time. That night they sat outside the cabin, and Jim talked about the forest and the ways of the forest creatures. He went over with Tom the most important things about trailing and trapping and making the most of what the forest could offer.

The next day Tom went back to town, but Jim said that he would stay on in the forest for a while. Tom spent the days getting the yard in shape and deciding what he would take to St. Louis. He really didn't mind going because it would be fun to see his friends there and tell them about the Choctaw country and about Jim. It was only when he thought about why he was going that the fun went out of it and he wondered whether going was the right thing to do.

One day before they were to leave for St. Louis, Isom Kincade rode into town. He stopped by to see Tom, and it made Tom feel proud that one of the famous light-horsemen would do that. Later that afternoon Tom saw Chief Jonathan Wolf in town. It was the first time that Tom could remember his ever having been there, and he felt in his bones that tomorrow was the day.

That night Jim rode back to the Baxter house. He looked rested and healthy, and it seemed to Tom that the whole strength and calm of the forest was in him.

"I didn't ask," he said, "but I hope you folks will put me up for the night."

"Your place is set at the table," Hannah Baxter said, "and your bed is made down."

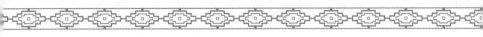

While they were sitting on the porch after supper, Billy Wakaya came by. "I think you're going to have some visitors in a few minutes, Jim," he said.

Jim frowned. "I don't want this evening to be upset," he said. "What is it?"

The sheriff said, "Some friends of yours. They still think they can keep your sentence from being carried out."

Jim shook his head. "Tell them not to come. Tell them to stop their scheming."

The sound of voices came through the night and Wakaya said, "Too late. They're here."

A dozen or more people came across the lawn and up to the porch. Jim stood up and waited for them. Tom was surprised to see several white people among the Indians. One of the Choctaws stepped forward a little and said, "Jim, we've come to tell you that we will stop this thing if you say the word. We claim it's not a legal sentence anymore, and we can get a hundred more around Atoka to back us up."

Jim looked at the group and said, "You are my friends. I can see all of you ,and I know that. Since you are my friends, I ask you to go home and say no more about this."

There were mumbles of protest in the crowd, and Jim continued, "You don't know what you are doing. If I let you stop the execution, the whole Choctaw Nation would take sides and there would be fighting. The enemies of our people would see their chance to do all the things they want to do. And I would be the one to blame. Do you think I want that?"

The crowd was silent, and Jim added, "I thank you. If you want to help me, say no more about this. Smile when I walk by tomorrow. I'll smile back."

They went away then, and Jim sat down. He said nothing about the people who had come but talked of small things

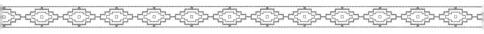

with Tom and his mother and father. After an hour he said, "The train comes early in the morning. We'd best go to bed. Tomorrow will be a big day for all of us."

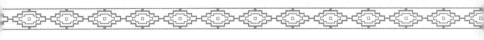

CHAPTER 15

When Tom slipped out of the house and into the backyard, the sky had cracked open, just a crease, beyond the eastern ridges; but in the pale light he could pick out the figure of Jim, who was standing with his head tilted toward the slit of brightness above the hills. Jim wore his best buckskin shirt. He had already been to the creek, and his face and hair gleamed. He said, "You're up early, Tom. Too excited about the trip to sleep?"

Tom had decided during the night to have it out, without wasting words. "I'm not going on any trip—at least not today."

Jim shook his head. "Today would be the best day to go, Tom. And your mother is all ready. You don't want to disappoint her."

"I think my mother won't mind waiting for the Wednesday train. Jim, I know what's going on. I know what's going to happen today. I couldn't leave town now. I know it might be easier on me that way, but—"

"It might be easier for all of us, Tom. Ever think of that?"

"I spent part of the night thinking of it. 'What's easy isn't always what's good.' You taught me that." Tom had saved one argument that he thought would be most important of all. He decided that the time had come to use it, but he hated

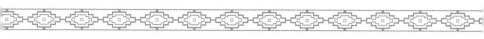

to mention it. He said, "Sending me away makes it look like you don't think I could stand up to things."

"No," Jim said, "I wouldn't want you to think that was it at all."

"Then I want to stay in Atoka today. I want to go along with you."

"You can't do that," Jim told him. "This is a Choctaw matter. They wouldn't let you, and I wouldn't want you. Once I walk through that town and meet Billy and Isom, it becomes a Choctaw matter."

"Then I could go with you that far—until you meet Billy and Isom."

Jim thought of that as the light grew and sharpened the lines of his face and forehead. "Getting on that train would be the easiest thing—"

Tom said nothing. He had stated his case. He knew it was up to Jim then. He had the feeling that Jim would understand the need for him to stay.

"All right," Jim agreed. "There's no law against friends walking through town with me. We'll meet Billy and Isom out by the stable. Then you and your father keep right on going out to my cabin. I left things out there for you. I'll go on my way with Billy and Isom." For just an instant Jim's face showed worry lines, and then it cleared as more sun came into the yard, and he said, "You'd better go in now and tell your mother about the change in plans."

Hannah Baxter was pan-frying slices of ham when Tom came into the kitchen, and without turning from the stove, she said, "Tom, we'd best get a move on if we're to make that train."

"Mom, I just talked to Jim. I explained to him why I can't take that train out today. I can't leave until after he rides out with Isom and Billy. I mean a friend wouldn't leave—"

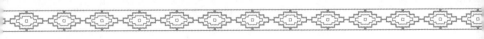

"When did you decide this?" Hannah Baxter asked.

"Last night. I thought it all out. Going out on that train wouldn't be right. We can still take the Wednesday train. After—"

"I'd rather we were on that train today," Hannah Baxter said. "I'd much rather that. What did Jim say when you told him?"

"The same as you. But he finally agreed that I could walk with him to the place where he meets Isom and Billy. He wants Pa to go along too."

Harvey Baxter had come into the kitchen behind Tom. He had stopped to listen, and he said nothing until Tom finished speaking. Hannah Baxter asked him, "What do you think, Harvey?"

"Maybe Tom is right. If he feels that it's his duty to stay." He faced Tom. "I want you to know this—I think you're old enough to know your own mind and to know what's right. I guess we'll walk out to meet Billy and Isom."

"All right," Hannah Baxter agreed. "Let's get breakfast on the table."

Tom crossed to his mother and squeezed her hard, trying to tell her without words how he felt. He realized that the change of plans would be hardest on her.

"Let's get breakfast on the table," Hannah said again.

They walked three abreast in the roadway where the dust had been laid by a heavy morning dew. The new day was cool, but it promised heat later, and Jim, who was sniffing the air as they walked, said, "It is likely to rain later."

"We could sure use some of that rain," Harvey Baxter remarked.

The remark delighted Jim for some reason. He nudged Tom and grinned. Jim moved rapidly on the roadway, looking all around as though he were out on a game scout up in the hills. It occurred to Tom that Jim was reaching out hungrily for that day, trying to take all of it in with his eyes and nose and ears, so that it could be stored in his heart as one last unbroken day. The thought that it was the last day troubled Tom, but the fact that Jim seemed to be getting so much out of the day made it seem better. Tom could understand that, and understanding that he could see why the Choctaws gave a man a year of freedom. It was up to the man to use it.

Jim turned suddenly and caught Tom thinking. Jim twitched his nostrils and said, "Raise up your head and tell me every scent that comes to you."

Tom said, "Pine from the ridges. Creek mud. Flowers from the gardens. Sawdust."

Jim said, "The important scent that I get is of grapes. That would make good walusha."

As they came to the outer edge of the town, they saw the first people waiting there, and Tom noticed that at first Jim was embarrassed and stared over the heads of the waiting people. Tom noticed too that many of the people were the same ones who had come out to the house before. They were doing what Jim had asked them to do, smiling as he walked by. The people stared at Jim openly and not out of the corners of their eyes or from behind half-pulled curtains. Jim's eyes came down to meet those of his friends. Mrs. Frieze called and waved, "Hello, Jim. Good luck now, ya hear?"

"A funny thing to say," Jim remarked. Then he thought a moment and said, "No, it's a good thing to say."

A pair of Kelly kids, tow-headed, freckled, and skinny like the rest of the Kellys, tagged behind them a few steps in the road, chattering and curious. Jim fished something from his shirt pocket. He turned and sent one coin, and then

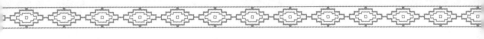

another spinning and shining, toward the children. They scrambled for them in the dust, caught them and called together, "Thankee, Mr. Jim."

Jim said, "These kids are learning some manners in this town." He was smiling.

Tom tried to face the smile and return it, but he couldn't. They had started down the last long stretch of the main street, and the thought of what waited at the other end hit Tom hard. He wondered if he were showing any of what he felt, and the thought bothered him so much that he turned away, blinking. He tried to take the day in as Jim had, and he looked all around and saw Gipson Bohanon lumbering through the scattered people, like a bear moving across a clearing of pine stumps. Gipson came out onto the roadway and made a sign to Jim. They turned to face each other, and they passed some message in Choctaw. They did not shake hands.

When Gipson turned his broad back and moved away, Tom felt sorrow coming back on him stronger than before, because Gipson's goodbye was a preview of what would happen when they reached the end of the street and he had to say goodbye to Jim. Tom fought to keep his face straight until after they had said the goodbye. There were only a few hundred yards to walk, and he straightened his shoulders and tried to force on a grin like the one Jim turned toward the people who watched him pass. Jim even had a grin and a nod for Roger Going, who waited in the middle of the crowd with some of his Progressive friends. Roger turned away.

Old man Weber and two Choctaw farmers came to the front of the feed store when Jim passed. The Indians said nothing, but old Weber called out, "Morning, Mr. Baxter. Morning, Mr. Moshulatubbee." Then, to Tom, Weber said a strange thing, "Good morning, Mr. Baxter."

Tom had begun to scuff along with his head down, but when Weber spoke to him, he straightened up and smiled,

and Jim said, "He knows there are three men walking by out here. You're doing fine, Tom."

There wasn't a buggy moving on the street. That meant somebody had arranged things beforehand, and the people along the roadway were there to see Jim walk past. Practically everyone in town was there. Tom saw Mr. Bronson and his wife in the crowd. When he saw them, Tom winced, thinking of how close he came to going out of town on the early train. If he had done that, he could never have faced the town again. There were things that had to be done by decent men.

In the middle of the crowd a woman began to cry. She was probably no one who knew Jim very well, just some-one who cried easily, but the sight of her bothered Tom. He turned away from her, and his head went down again.

Once they had reached the end of the street and turned into the woods toward Jim's cabin, Tom wouldn't care how he looked or what happened to him. Only his father would see him then, and he knew that his father understood. His father seemed to sense something was wrong. He turned in the street and nodded encouragement, and Tom managed to nod to show that everything was all right with him.

They moved through the shadows of store fronts and across splashes of sun at the entrances to alleys and cross-lanes. Far down the street Tom could see two men waiting in the shadow of the livery stable. He could see their white hats, even in the shadows, but their faces under the hat brims were too weathered and Indian to show any clear features. Still, Tom knew that Billy Wakaya and Isom Kincade were waiting there, and the sight of them stopped him dead in his tracks.

He shuffled in the dust and might even have turned and run—he didn't know where to—if his father hadn't reached out to lay a heavy hand on his shoulder and gentle him for-ward. Tom turned to see if Jim had noticed, but Jim was too

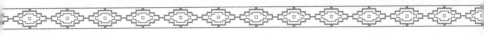

busy noticing the people who had come out to greet him. To
Jim those people were important, Tom realized. It wasn't that
Jim was trying to glorify himself or prove that he was brave.
Jim was out to give a lesson in Choctaw honor to Indians and
whites, and to show them how important he thought the laws
of his Nation were.

Halfway to the stable there was a buggy, all alone by the
roadside, and in it sat Jonathan Wolf, Principal Chief of the
Choctaws. When he saw the buggy, Tom's heart began to
beat rapidly. In that buggy waited Jim's last chance for life.
Tom searched the Chief's face for any sign of what was to
come. The Chief's face was calm, and his corded hands were
folded quietly over the buggy reins; he waited, unblinkingly,
as Jim moved toward him. The Chief looked powerful, but
lonely, waiting there.

Tom made a sudden quick dash forward, trying to get
up to where Jim had stopped beside the buggy. There was
a chance—there was just a chance. Jim had stopped and
swung to face the Chief, Tom noticed. Perhaps Jim felt there
was a chance too.

The Chief's face showed nothing as Jim began to speak
to him in Choctaw. Jim spoke only a few words, and the
Chief said nothing. The silence that followed frightened Tom
because he could understand nothing of what had passed between the two men. Finally, deliberately, the Chief muttered
a word or two and nodded. To Tom's surprise, Jim began to
move on past the buggy, and Tom had to run a step to catch
up to him.

"What did you say to him?" Tom asked.

"I thanked him," Jim said.

"Thanked him for what?"

"For what he has done for the Choctaws. For what I hope
he will do."

"But what did he do for you?"

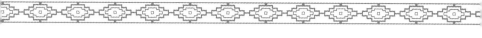

"There's nothing he can do for me. There's nothing that I want him to do for me. Our law has spoken on me."

"Then why did he come here? Why did he make me think—"

"He came for the same reason that I came here—that you came here. It would have been easier for him to stay away. But this was his duty." They were only ten yards away from the stable where Billy and Isom waited. In a low voice, Jim said, "If you ever felt sorry for anyone, feel sorry for them. There are two of the best friends I have in this world." Jim raised his voice then and called, "Billy, Isom—I'm here." Then he said something to them in Choctaw.

Isom Kincade and Billy Wakaya shuffled forward into the sunny street. Neither man wore a weapon, and Tom was glad of that. Billy, as usual, had his pant legs tied down to his boot tops, and the baggy trousers made his legs look extra bowed. His face was seamed and cracked from riding through a hundred storms and under a thousand strong suns. If he felt anything toward Jim, he didn't show it. Tom knew that Billy must feel something for Jim. They had been friends since boyhood. Tom tried to keep his face like Billy's. It was almost over.

Kincade came forward. His face was weathered but not as lined as Billy's. He showed nothing in his face, but he was holding a willow switch, and Tom could see that it was gripped tighter than it had to be.

Jim said in English, "You know the Baxters, Tom and Harvey."

The way Jim said it surprised Tom. It was the first time he remembered anyone introducing him as though he were a grown man like his father. Tom felt himself begin to tremble, and he shook his head hard, fighting for control. If they were treating him like a man, he had to act like one. He wished

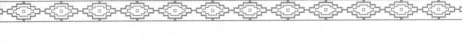

that he had something to grip hard on, like the willow switch that Isom carried.

Isom and Billy nodded to the Baxters, and they all shuffled a moment in the dusty street. Behind the high door of the stable a horse nickered and pawed and hit the side of his stall a whack.

"That your pony raising a fuss in there?" Jim asked Kincade.

Isom grinned and shook his head. "We left the horses out the road a ways. Yours is there too." Even as he grinned, Isom was gripping the willow switch hard.

Tom had to glance away from the sight of Isom's grip on the switch. It told so much about what Isom was feeling.

"You ready, Jim?" Billy asked.

"Yes."

Tom heard the sound of the switch breaking in Isom's hands. The last day broke with it.

Jim turned quickly then and shook Harvey Baxter's hand. Then he had Tom's hand before there was time to realize what was going on. It was the first time Jim had ever shaken hands with him, and the shock of it drove every other thought out of Tom's mind. As he squeezed, Jim said simply, "Tom," and then turned away without another word.

Jim and Isom and Billy were speaking Choctaw as they moved away. They were soon out of Tom's hearing, and he never did look up to watch them go.

Tom felt his father touch his arm and he heard him say, "Let's go, Tom. Jim wanted us to go along to his cabin."

Tom held his face firm until they reached the edge of the woods. Then he twisted back toward his father and said, "Do you mind if I run ahead?"

"No, go ahead. Go ahead. I'll meet you at the cabin."

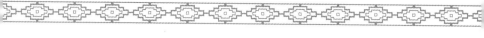

He ran with his head high through a grove of pines where the going was easy and came out in a cleared space where branch stubs on the high stumps tore at his clothes and scratched his hands. Still running hard, he slipped through a thicket of scrub oak and came stumbling down through rushes to the edge of a stream where he floundered and fell. He rose, with mud staining his arms and face, and churned up over a brushy hill. When he reached the top of the rise, he charged down into a swale of bramble and vine. The bramble and vine forced him to lower his head, but he drove through the thicket with the thorns tearing at his neck and hands. Beyond the thicket was a moss-bottomed swamp, and there pain took him in the chest as he lost his first wind trying to run hard through the soft mud. He fell again, feeling pain in his legs and arms from the bramble scratches and more pain in his heart. But still he felt relief because he realized that he had reached a place where he could cry if he had to.

Before he went to the cabin, he stopped at the creek and washed the swamp mud from his hands and the stains of sweat and tears from his face. After undressing, he washed off all the dried blood. Then he plunged into the clear cold water and thrashed up a great foam with his arms and legs. When he dressed, he rolled down the sleeves of his shirt so the bramble scratches would not show.

He remembered how calm and strong and gleaming clean Jim had always looked after a swim in the creek, and he hoped he looked like that as he walked in to meet his father.